Praise for

DEAD VOICES

★ "Arden's high scare factor, richly drawn mountain setting, relevant themes of loss and belonging, and vividly eerie descriptions evoke the very best of horror for this age set."

—*Kirkus Reviews*, starred review

"This chilling sequel to *Small Spaces* . . . [has all] the necessary trappings for a classic ghost story."   —*The Horn Book*

★ "Arden handily transforms the haunted house story into something much richer, scarier, and more sinister . . . Middle-graders who thrill to spooks and scares will find plenty (maybe even more than they bargained for!) here."

—*Booklist*, starred review

"Entertaining and will be enjoyed by middle school fans of light horror."   —*VOYA*

★ "In this spooky sequel to *Small Spaces*, Arden excels at creating an atmosphere of claustrophobic tension with memorably menacing details. Readers will again be invested in the ghoulish surprises in store for the resourceful, likably flawed protagonists."
—*Publishers Weekly*, starred review

"Standing just fine on its own (though newcomers will definitely be inspired to read *Small Spaces*), this is a fine addition to any scary stories shelf."   —*School Library Journal*

Praise for

SMALL SPACES

"Is it a mystery? A fairy tale? A horror thriller? As the suspense gripped me, I just wanted to know one thing—WHAT HAPPENS NEXT? Terrifying and fun."　　　　—R. L. Stine, author of the Goosebumps and Fear Street series

"Irresistibly spooky."　　　　　　　　　　　—*Entertainment Weekly*

★ "Atmospheric horror at its best. Chillingly tender."
　　　　　　　　　　　　—*Kirkus Reviews*, starred review

"The perfect book to be read by firelight during a chilly autumn evening—though you might find yourself inching closer to the light as the story nears its terrifying conclusion. Katherine Arden is a gifted storyteller with a wicked imagination!"

—J. A. White, author of The Thickety series and *Nightbooks*

"This book scared the snot out of me. Fast-paced and spine-tinglingly delightful. I defy you to read the first two chapters without staying up the rest of the night to finish. You've been warned!"　　　　　　　　—Jonathan Auxier, *New York Times* bestselling author of *The Night Gardener*

DEAD VOICES

ALSO BY KATHERINE ARDEN

Small Spaces

The Winter of the Witch

The Girl in the Tower

The Bear and the Nightingale

DEAD VOICES

KATHERINE ARDEN

PUFFIN BOOKS

PUFFIN BOOKS
An imprint of Penguin Random House LLC, New York

First published in the United States of America by G. P. Putnam's Sons, 2019
Published by Puffin Books, an imprint of Penguin Random House LLC, 2020

Visit us online at penguinrandomhouse.com

THE LIBRARY OF CONGRESS HAS CATALOGED THE G. P. PUTNAM'S SONS EDITION AS FOLLOWS:
Names: Arden, Katherine, author.
Title: Dead voices / Katherine Arden.
Description: New York: G. P. Putnam's Sons, [2019] | Sequel to: Small spaces. |
Summary: "Trapped at a haunted ski resort, Ollie, Coco, and Brian must rely on their friendship and sharp minds if they want to escape"—Provided by publisher.
Identifiers: LCCN 2019014459 (print) | LCCN 2019017773 (ebook) | ISBN 9780525515067 (ebook) | ISBN 9780525515050 (hardback)
Subjects: | CYAC: Haunted places—Fiction. | Best friends—Fiction. | Friendship—Fiction. | Skis and skiing—Fiction. | Resorts—Fiction. | Survival—Fiction. | BISAC: JUVENILE FICTION / Action & Adventure / Survival Stories. | JUVENILE FICTION / Mysteries & Detective Stories. Classification: LCC PZ7.1.A737 (ebook) | LCC PZ7.1.A737 De 2019 (print) | DDC [Fic]—dc23
LC record available at https://lccn.loc.gov/2019014459

Puffin Books ISBN 9780525515074

Printed in the United States of America

Design by Eileen Savage
Text set in Dante MT Pro

5 7 9 10 8 6

To Garrett

Friend, housemate, pretty-much-sibling

Because I did promise you a cameo in this book

But I never said you'd be one of the good guys

DEAD VOICES

1

WINTER IN EAST EVANSBURG, and just after dusk, five people in a beat-up old Subaru peeled out of town in a snowstorm. Snow and road salt flew up from their tires as they got on the highway heading north. The five were nearly the only people on the road. *"A major winter storm is blanketing parts of northern Vermont with eight inches over-night . . ."* said the radio, crackling. *"Be advised that the roads are dangerous."*

The Subaru kept going. In front were two adults. In the back were three kids.

Coco Zintner sat in the middle of the back seat, because she was the smallest. She was short and skinny, her eyes blue, her hair (Coco's favorite thing about herself) an odd pinkish blond. Coco peered nervously through the windshield. The road looked slippery. They were going to spend the next three hours driving on it.

"Awesome," said the girl to Coco's left. Her name was Olivia Adler. She was Coco's best friend, and she wasn't nervous at all. "Eight inches overnight." She pressed her nose to the car window. She had big dark eyes and the kind of corkscrewing curls that couldn't ever be brushed, because they'd frizz. She stared out at the snowstorm with delight. "We're going to have so much fun tomorrow."

Coco's other best friend, the boy on Coco's right, grinned back at Ollie. The Subaru's storage area was piled high with bags. He reached into the jumble and patted his green ski boots. "It's gonna be *lit*," he said. "Don't look so nervous, Tiny."

That was to Coco. She scowled. Brian gave nearly everyone a nickname. She liked Brian, but she hated her nickname. Probably because she was actually kind of tiny. Brian had the best smile of anyone Coco knew. He'd been born in Jamaica, but his parents had moved to Vermont when he was a baby. He was black, not particularly tall, and the star of the middle school hockey team. He loved books as much as he loved scoring goals, and even though he could sometimes act like a dumb hockey player, Brian was good at noticing what went on around him.

Like the fact that Coco was nervous. She wished he wouldn't tease her about it.

It was the first day of winter break, and the five of them were going skiing: Ollie and Brian and Coco, plus

Ollie's dad (who was driving) and Coco's mom (who was riding shotgun).

Neither adult could really afford a week of skiing. Coco's mother was a journalist, and Ollie's father sold solar panels. But the month before, Ollie's dad had come home from work smiling.

"What?" Ollie had asked. She and Coco were sitting in the kitchen of the Egg, Ollie's rambling old farmhouse. They'd gotten themselves mugs of hot chocolate and were seeing who could build the biggest marshmallow pyramid on top.

Mr. Adler just grinned. "Want to go skiing over the winter holiday?"

"Huh?" said both girls in chorus.

Turned out Ollie's dad had won a prize. For selling a lot of solar panels. A week for him and four others at Mount Hemlock.

"Mount Hemlock?" Ollie had asked, stunned. "But it's not even open yet!"

Mount Hemlock was Vermont's newest ski mountain. It had never been open to the public before. Some school had owned it. But now it had new owners, who were turning the mountain into a winter getaway.

"Yep," said Mr. Adler happily. "They're hosting a few people over the holiday, before the official opening. Want to go? Coco? Do you and your mom want to go?"

Coco had only learned to ski that winter, and still thought that sliding fast down a mountain was cold and scary. She wasn't sure if she wanted to go. But Ollie was already doing a happy dance around the house, and Coco didn't want to disappoint her.

"Sure," she said in a small voice. "Yeah, I'll go."

Now they were actually in the car, actually going, and Coco had butterflies in her stomach, thinking of the storm, the slippery road, the big cold mountain at the end of it. She wished they were still back at Ollie's house, in front of Bernie the woodstove, making marshmallow pyramids. The wind whipped snow across the windshield.

Coco told Brian, in a voice that probably fooled no one, "I'm not nervous about *skiing*." She waved a hand at the windshield. "I'm nervous about driving in a snowstorm."

"Well," said Mr. Adler calmly from the front, "technically, *I'm* driving in a snowstorm." He changed gears on the Subaru. His hair was as dark as Ollie's, though it was straight instead of curly. For the winter, he'd grown out a giant reddish beard. *Keeps me warm,* he would say.

"You're doing amazing, Dad," Ollie said. "You and Susie." Susie was the Subaru. "Dad's driven through a lot of snowstorms," she said to Coco reassuringly. "All fine."

The streetlights disappeared a little outside of Evansburg, and it was dark on the road except for their headlights.

"It's okay, Tiny," said Brian. "We probably won't slide into a ditch."

"Probably?" Coco asked.

"Definitely," said Coco's mom from the passenger seat. She turned back to give Brian a stern look. Brian played innocent. Coco and her mom had the exact same blue eyes, though her mom was tall instead of tiny, and her hair was blond, not pinkish. Coco kept hoping for a growth spurt.

"If we do slide into a ditch," said Ollie, "you get to push us out, Brian."

"Naw," said Brian. "You're bigger than me. You push us out."

Coco interrupted. "You both can push us out. Are there any snacks?"

That distracted all three of them. It was dinnertime, and there were snacks. Mr. Adler was a specialist in snacks. He'd made them each a large peanut-butter-and-jelly sandwich on homemade bread.

After they'd finished their sandwiches, they each ate an apple and shared a big bag of potato chips. Mr. Adler had made the chips too.

"Is it *hard* to make potato chips?" Coco asked disbelievingly, licking salt off her fingers.

"No," said Ollie, in a superior tone. She'd helped make

them. Also, Coco suspected, eaten a lot of them before the drive even started. "But the oil splashes."

"I know what we're making next time we're at your house," said Brian, crunching. "These are *amazing*."

They were scuffling over the last of the potato chips when the Subaru finally turned off the main highway. MOUNTAIN ACCESS ROAD, said a sign. The road tilted steeply up. On one side were trees. On the other side was a gully and a frozen creek. Ollie's dad was driving on through the storm like he didn't have a care in the world, telling bad jokes from the front seat.

"What did the buffalo say to his kid when he dropped him off at school?" he asked.

Ollie sighed. Her dad *loved* bad jokes.

"Bison!" yelped Coco triumphantly, and everyone groaned but also laughed.

"*Motorists are warned to exercise caution, avoid unplowed roads, and, if at all possible, refrain from driving altogether,*" remarked the radio.

"Great," said Mr. Adler, unbothered. "Less people on the road tonight means more snow for us tomorrow!"

"If you say so," said Coco's mom. She gave the smothering storm a cautious look. Coco recognized the look. Coco and her mom were both careful about things. Unlike Ollie and her dad, who were kind of leap-before-you-look.

"Want to hear another joke?" Mr. Adler asked.

"Dad, can't we have a jokes-per-trip limit?" Ollie said.

"Not when I'm driving!" said her dad. "One more. Why did the scarecrow get a promotion?"

A small, awkward silence fell. Ollie, Brian, and Coco looked at each other. They *really* didn't like scarecrows.

"Anyone?" asked Ollie's dad. "Anyone? Come on, I feel like I'm talking to myself here! Because he was *outstanding in his field*! Get it? Out standing in his field?" Ollie's dad laughed, but no one laughed with him. "Geez, tough crowd."

The three in the back said nothing. Ollie's dad didn't know it, but there was a reason they didn't like scarecrows.

That October, they, along with the rest of their sixth-grade class, had disappeared for two days. Only Ollie, Brian, and Coco remembered everything that had happened during those days. They'd never told anyone. They told their families and the police that they'd gotten lost.

They hadn't just gotten lost. But who would believe them if they told the truth?

They'd been kidnapped into another world. A world behind the mist. They'd met living scarecrows who tried to drag them off and turn them into scarecrows too. They'd gone into a haunted house, taken food from a ghost, run a corn maze, and at last met someone called the smiling man.

The smiling man looked ordinary, but he wasn't. The smiling man would grant your heart's desire if you asked him. But he'd demand a price. A terrible price.

Ollie, Brian, and Coco had outwitted the smiling man. They'd survived the world behind the mist and come home. They'd gone into that world as near strangers and come out as best friends. It was December now, and they were together, and on vacation. All was well.

But two months later, they still had nightmares. And they still didn't like scarecrows.

The silence in the car stretched out as the road got even steeper. The radio suddenly fizzed with static and went silent.

They all waited for it to crackle back to life. Nothing. Coco's mom reached out and tapped it, pressed the tuning button, but it didn't help. "That's weird," she said. "Maybe it's the storm."

Coco didn't miss the radio. She was full of peanut butter and getting sleepy. She leaned her head on Ollie's shoulder to doze. Brian was reading *Voyage of the Dawn Treader*. Brian liked sea stories. He and Ollie had both read one called *Captain Blood* and spent a few weeks arguing about the ending. Coco had read the book too, to know what her friends were arguing about, but it was about pirates. She hadn't liked it and felt a little left out of the whole argument. Coco didn't like novels, really. She liked books about real things. Bugs and dinosaurs and the history of space flight.

Brian began to read by the light of his phone. Ollie put her cheek against her window and stared into the wild night. Coco, half asleep on Ollie's shoulder, began recalling the last chess game she'd played. It was on the internet, with someone named @begemot.

Coco loved chess. Her favorite books were histories of famous players and famous matches. One of her favorite things to do was to play online. On the internet, no one could be smug and assume she was easy to beat just because she was small and pink-haired. Sleepily, Coco went back over the opening moves of her last game. She'd played white, which always goes first, and had opened with Queen's Gambit . . .

Up and up they climbed.

Coco fell asleep, still thinking about chess.

Coco dreamed. Not about chess.

In her dream, she was walking down a dark hallway, so long that she couldn't see the end of it. Bars of moonlight fell across the carpet, striping it with shadows. But there weren't any windows. Just the moonlight. It was bitterly cold. On each side were rows of plain white doors, the paint rotten and peeling. Behind one of the doors, Coco heard someone crying.

But behind which door? There seemed to be hundreds. "Where are you?" Coco called.

"I can't find them," whimpered a girl's voice. "I've looked everywhere, but I can't find them. Mother says I can't go home until I find them."

Coco thought she heard footsteps plodding along behind her. Heavy, uneven footsteps. Her skin started to crawl. But she had to find the crying girl. She was sure of it. She had to find her before the footsteps caught up. She ran along faster. "What are you looking for?" she called. "I can help you find it. Where are you?"

Then she lurched to a halt. A skinny girl, about her own height, dressed in a white nightgown, had appeared in the hallway. Her face was in shadow. "Here," the girl said.

For some reason, Coco did not want to see the girl's face. "Hello?" she said, hearing her voice crack.

"I'm looking for my bones," whispered the girl. "Can you help me?"

She moved into the light. Coco flinched. The other girl was gray-faced and skinny. Her eyes were two blank pits. Her lips and nose were black, like she had terrible frostbite. She tried, horribly, to smile. "Hello," she said.

"It's cold here, isn't it? Won't you help me?" She reached out a single hand. Her fingernails were long and black in the moonlight.

Coco, stumbling backward, ran into something solid. A huge hand fell on her shoulder. Coco whirled and looked up into the face of a scarecrow. Its sewn-on mouth was smiling wide. Its hand wasn't a hand at all, just a sharp garden trowel. It had found her at last, Coco thought. It had found her, and now it was going to drag her off. She'd never get home again . . .

Coco opened her mouth to scream, and woke up with a gasp.

She was in the car, in the snowstorm, driving to Mount Hemlock, and her mother was talking to Mr. Adler in the front seat. It was cold in the back seat; her toes in their winter boots were numb. Coco sat still for a second, breathing fast with fright. *Just a dream,* she told herself. She'd had a lot of scarecrow dreams in the last few months. So had Ollie and Brian. *Just a dream.*

"How much farther, Roger?" Coco's mom asked.

"Should be pretty close now," said Mr. Adler.

Coco, a little dazed from her nightmare, stared out the front windshield. It was snowing even harder. The road was a thin yellowish-white strip, piled thick with snow. More snow bowed the trees on either side.

The Subaru was moving slowly. The thick snow groaned under the wheels, and Mr. Adler seemed to be struggling to keep the car going straight on the slippery road. "What a night, huh?" he said.

"Want me to drive?" asked Coco's mom.

This time the usual cheer was gone from Mr. Adler's reply. "It's okay. I know the car better." Lower, he added, "Just pray we don't get stuck."

Now the car was coming down into a gully, the road turning slightly.

But the road wasn't empty. For a stomach-clenching second, Coco thought she was still dreaming. Right in front of them, in the middle of the road, stood a tall figure in a ragged blue ski jacket. It looked like a scarecrow. The figure was perfectly still. One palm was raised and turned out as though to beg. As though to say, *STOP*. The face was hidden by a ski mask.

Coco felt a jolt of terror. But then she realized that the person had real hands. Not garden tools. She wasn't dreaming; this wasn't a scarecrow.

Mr. Adler wasn't slowing down. "Stop!" yelled Coco, yanking herself upright. "Look! *Look!*"

Mr. Adler slammed on the brakes. The car skidded, turning sideways, swinging them toward the thick black ranks of trees. Coco braced, waiting to hear the thump of someone slamming into the side of the car. The person had been *so close* . . .

Nothing.

The car shuddered to a stop, only a couple feet from the nearest tree trunk.

All of them sat stunned for a second.

"I didn't feel us hit anything." Mr. Adler sounded like he was taking deep breaths, trying to be calm. "What did you see, Coco?"

Coco was startled. "You didn't see it? There was a person in the road! We must have hit him!" Her voice sounded squeaky. She hated when her voice sounded squeaky. Had they hurt someone? Had they *killed* . . .

Ollie's dad put on the emergency brake and turned on the car's hazard lights. "Kids, I need you to stay—" he began, but Ollie had already unlocked her door and scrambled out into the snow. It came up to her knees. Brian was right behind her on his side, and Coco, although her hands were shaking, hurried after them.

"Coco!" cried her mom as she and Mr. Adler followed. "Coco, don't look, get back, be careful—"

Coco pretended not to hear. She grabbed her phone, went around the car, and shined the light at the snow. Brian was doing the same. Ollie had pulled a headlamp from the pocket on her car door. The three of them stood shoulder to shoulder, shining their flashlights all around the car. The snow was falling so thickly that they couldn't see anything outside the circle of their lights. Faintly, Coco heard the whisper of wind in the pine needles overhead.

Mr. Adler had a flashlight from the glove compartment. Coco's mom stood next to him, squinting into the snowstorm. Four beams of light shone on the snow. The road was utterly empty. Coco saw the tracks where the car had come down, saw the huge sideways mark of the car's skid. But nothing else.

"I don't see anyone. Any tracks, even," said her mom. "Thank god."

"But I *saw* someone," protested Coco. "In the road. A person. They had their hand out." She raised her own arm, palm out, to demonstrate. "They were wearing a blue ski jacket, but no gloves. Ollie, did you see?"

"I thought I might have seen something," said Ollie. She sounded doubtful. "Like a shadow. But I wasn't sure. There's so much snow. Brian?"

Brian shook his head. "But," he said loyally, "Ollie and I couldn't see out the windshield as well as Coco, since she was in the middle."

Coco's mom gestured at the snow, which was unmarked except for the car's tracks and their own footprints. "I don't think there was anyone here." She started to shiver.

They'd all taken off their heavy coats for driving, and now the snow was piling up on their shoulders.

"I *saw* someone," Coco insisted, but the others, eager to get back into the warm car, weren't listening anymore. She hurried after them. "I definitely saw someone."

"It might have just been a shadow, Tiny," said Brian reasonably. "Or a deer. Or maybe you were just dreaming and you mixed up being asleep and being awake."

"I wasn't imagining things!" cried Coco, wishing *so hard* that her voice wouldn't squeak. "And don't call me Tiny!"

"But there's obviously no one—" Brian began.

"Hey," said Ollie's dad, cutting them off. "Easy now, both of you. Just be glad we didn't hit anyone. Let's get back in the car. It's not safe here."

Coco climbed unhappily back into the car. She felt like everyone was just a little bit mad at her for yelling *stop* so that Mr. Adler had to slam on his brakes and send them skidding dangerously across the road. She was *sure* she'd seen someone.

But she *had* been half asleep. Maybe she did dream it.

As they drove away, Coco turned around and looked out the back window.

Just for a second, she thought she saw a dark figure lit red by the car's rear lights. It stood facing them in the middle of the road. One bare hand was still upraised.

Like a plea.

Like a warning.

"Guys," she whispered. "It's there. It's *right back there*."

Ollie and Brian turned around.

There was a small silence.

"I don't see anything," said Ollie.

Coco looked again.

The figure was gone.

Coco shivered. She opened her mouth to say something else. But before she could, the car was grumbling up the mountain once more and they had left the gully behind them.

A minute later, two yellow lights shone through the trees. Maybe it was just because Coco was shaken up, but she thought that the lights looked sinister. Like eyes peeping. Waiting for them. She wanted to tell Mr. Adler to turn the car around.

Don't be silly, she told herself.

"Look!" said Brian, pointing. "What's that?"

"Must be the lodge," said Mr. Adler. He sounded relieved. "We're almost there."

They drove under a new, hand-carved sign lit by two old-fashioned gas lamps.

Eyes? Right, Coco thought. *Just lamps.*

MOUNT HEMLOCK RESORT, said the sign. A MOUNTAIN OF AWESOME WHERE WINTER NEVER ENDS.

"That's some weird grammar," commented Ollie.

No one said anything else. The resort drive was the narrowest road they'd driven on, and the most thickly piled with snow. The Subaru's motor whined horribly as Ollie's dad pushed down the accelerator. The driveway turned, and the car skidded slowly sideways, almost going into a spin. The wheels couldn't bite.

"Dad—" Ollie began.

"Not now!" snapped her father in a tone Coco had never heard from Mr. Adler. He changed gears, managed to keep the car from skidding, and then they burst out from the driveway into a snow-covered parking lot. Everyone breathed a huge sigh of relief.

After the long, cold drive, the sight of Hemlock Lodge was like Christmas morning. Warm golden light blazed out of the windows. Well, some of the windows.

"We made it," said Brian happily.

They could barely see the building in the snowy darkness, but Coco thought it was big. It had a—presence. It loomed over them.

"Shouldn't there be more lights?" asked Ollie.

"Power must be out," said Coco's mom. She tugged the end of her blond braid, considering. "They're running on generators. Can't light everything."

"I can hear the generators," said Brian.

Mr. Adler drove across the parking lot and parked

under an awning. Coco could hear the generators too: a slow, roaring noise, like the building was breathing.

"Well," said Mr. Adler, "parking lot's empty. Looks like we were the only ones to make the drive."

"There might be others stuck on the road some-where," said Coco's mom. "Hopefully they get to shelter. Another hour, and we'd have gotten stuck ourselves. Next time let's listen to what the radio has to say about snow-storms, hm?"

"Deal," said Ollie's dad, and he sounded like he really meant it. "Come on!" he added to all of them. "We made it, all present and accounted for. Grab a bag. The sooner we get out, the sooner we get to bed."

Ollie and Brian fumbled for the door handles and stumbled into the freezing night. All of them padded sleepily into Hemlock Lodge.

Coco stopped dead right in the entrance, staring. Ollie plowed into Coco and had to catch her so they both didn't fall. "Coco, what—" she began, and then she saw what Coco had. "No way."

"Holy cow," muttered Brian. "Where are we?"

The only light in the lobby was from a big, roaring fire. Shadows leaped and swung across the walls; you couldn't even see the ceiling. But the walls were completely covered with heads. Dead animal heads. Coco spotted a moose head with Christmas lights wound through its antlers. A deer head—a lot of deer heads—hung in a cluster. There was a trio of raccoons in a small canoe with paddles. A stuffed fawn in a glass box. Four coyotes looked like they were howling at a fake moon. A black bear stood on its hind legs, its paw upraised.

In the flickering firelight, they seemed to move; their glass eyes shone like they were alive. The bear had sharp white teeth.

"Nice decorations," said Brian uneasily. "Great spot your dad found." There was a giant bearskin rug on the floor. Its claws were shiny in the firelight.

Ollie stepped around Coco and marched into the lobby. "It's great," she said pointedly. Ollie always defended her dad. Coco would have too, if she'd had a dad as cool as Ollie's. Coco had never met her dad. He'd left before Coco was born.

Ollie waved at the heads. "Some people like this kind of thing. And we're not here to hang out in the lobby, we're here to ski."

Brian brightened. "Yes, we are," he said. His green ski boots were draped over his backpack; he reached behind and patted them again. Brian loved all gear, for all sports. Especially his own gear. He and Ollie would go on endlessly about tuning skis and sharpening ice skates. Sometimes

Coco wished that she liked the things her friends liked. Pirate books and winter stuff. She'd have more to say when they were talking.

Two people, a man and a woman, had been standing by the front desk, waiting for them. Now they hurried forward, clattering across the lodge. They were smiling, freckled, happy. Coco was really glad to see them. They made the lobby seem a lot more normal.

"Oh, you made it, I'm so glad!" said the woman. She was thin as a greyhound, sandy-haired, with *cheery welcome* written all over her face like she'd painted it there. "You must be Roger Adler," she said to Ollie's dad. "I'm Sue Wilson. You're the first guests to arrive—a lot of them probably didn't set out at all! *What* a storm! Sorry about the dark." She waved a hand at the lobby. "We thought the fire would be enough. Electricity's out, and we're trying to save on propane in case we're snowed in for a couple of days. Plenty of firewood, though!" She turned to the kids. "You can call me Sue." She smiled at Coco. "You tired, hon?"

Coco was used to adults calling her *hon*, *sweetie*, and *darling*. Adults who didn't know her mostly seemed to think she was about eight years old. It was the pinkish hair. She *really* wished she'd get that growth spurt.

"Yes," she said politely, gritting her teeth. "I am. What happened to the electricity?"

"The storm," said the man, coming forward. "Wind blew trees over the power lines somewhere or other." He had a beard as big as Mr. Adler's and wore a Christmas sweater. A little belly hung over his belt. "I'm Sam Wilson," he said. "Me 'n' Sue own the place. Pleased to meet you. I guess you saw my little critters." He waved a hand at the wall. "Bagged 'em all myself! Lemme take those." He swept up all three of their duffels before they could respond. "Now," he said. "Enough chitchat. You must be tired. Stairs are this way. Sorry the elevator's not working. Power's out and all. Come on. Welcome to Hemlock Lodge."

Coco followed him gratefully, glad to get to bed and away from the animal heads.

"Big storm out there, Sue," Coco heard Mr. Adler saying. "Should make for some good skiing tomorrow, but it was a tough drive." He raised his voice. "Good night, kids! Be good."

The adults kept on talking, but Coco couldn't hear what they were saying. She padded up the stairs with the others.

They stopped on the second floor. The stairs opened onto a long dim hall. The only light was from a few wide-spaced wall lamps. They cast pools of feeble yellow light. *Must be part of saving on propane,* Coco decided, *keeping it so dark.* She tripped over the last step and lurched into Ollie,

21

who was weighed down by her own backpack and nearly went over.

"Coco!" whispered Ollie. She didn't usually get mad when Coco was clumsy, but they were all really tired.

"Sorry," Coco whispered back. "It's hard to see."

They began the long trudge down the hall. Coco watched her feet carefully, trying not to trip again. "I've got you girls in the bunk room," Sam called over his shoulder. "You"—Brian was it—"are right across the hall. Far end of the hallway. Follow me."

The hall seemed to go on forever. It was chilly. Coco hoped their room was warmer.

Sam stopped at a door that said BUNK ROOM in big brass letters.

Behind her, Coco heard more footsteps coming up the stairs, shuffling along behind them. Must be her mom and Mr. Adler, going to their rooms. Coco looked back. "Good night, Mo—" she started to say.

But her mom wasn't there. The hall was empty.

No—what was that? Near them was a pool of greenish light, thrown from one of the dim emergency bulbs. Cast across the light was a person's shadow. A big broad-shouldered shadow.

One shadow-hand was stretched out toward them.

Like a plea.

Like a warning.

A chill ran down her spine. "Mom?" Coco called just as their door swung open; Sam flicked on a battery-powered lamp. Light flooded the hall, and the shadow vanished. There was *definitely* no one there.

Coco thought then of the strange figure in the road and, for some reason, of the long hallway in her dream.

Her heart beating uncomfortably fast, Coco followed Ollie into the bunk room.

2

"BATHROOM'S JUST DOWN the hall," said Sam, pointing back the way they'd come. "Hope you guys like it in here. What a snowstorm, huh?"

It was. Ollie was glad they'd made it. She was even happier about their room. The bunk room was a lot warmer than the hallway. The lamp shed a bright, golden light. The walls were painted a cheerful yellow, with a wooden bunk bed, red blankets, a rocking chair, and a big mirror over a dresser. Pictures of skiing bears hung on the walls.

Ollie dropped her backpack by the dresser, knelt, and began digging around for a toothbrush and pajamas. "Want the top bunk?" she asked Coco. Coco loved climbing and being up high. Ollie hoped the top bunk would make her friend feel better. Coco was still looking worried.

"Yeah," said Coco gratefully. "That'd be great." She unzipped her own bag.

"You girls sleep well," said Sam from the doorway. "Need anything else?"

Ollie and Coco shook their heads.

"Night," said Brian, and he and Sam both went across the hall to Brian's room. Ollie closed the door behind them.

"Should we brush our teeth?" Coco asked. She didn't look excited about going back into the dark, chilly hall. Ollie wasn't either. But she didn't like having fuzzy teeth.

"In a sec. Wait for it," said Ollie.

"Wait for what?"

"Three, two . . ."

Brian popped back into their room.

"Right on time," said Ollie.

"Mr. Wilson's gone back downstairs," said Brian. "What do you guys think? About the lodge, I mean. I think it's kind of freaky." He sat down on the lower bunk bed. "I mean—those heads?"

"I think it's freaky too!" said Coco. "I saw—" She bit her tongue and sat down on the rocking chair without finishing her sentence. "Never mind," she muttered. "Just a shadow."

"Lodge seems great," said Ollie firmly, still digging into her bag. "Well, except for the heads. I'm with you on that." She pulled out a box of her dad's cookies and

25

passed them around. "These will make you feel better. The Wilsons seem nice. It's not their fault the power is out."

"But it's so *dark*," said Coco. She took a cookie. "Couldn't they have more generators? To make it less dark?"

"They're trying to save on propane. Like Mrs. Wilson told us," Ollie said reasonably.

"Hope we can ski tomorrow," said Brian. He was on his feet again, at the window, peering out like he was straining to see the ski mountain through the storm. Brian *loved* to ski. "Listen to that wind." Ski lifts could operate on backup generators, but not in high winds.

They all went silent, chewing their cookies. The wind had a voice. It whined and howled and whispered around Hemlock Lodge. Ollie saw Coco shiver. She'd never been totally on board with the skiing. That was okay, Ollie told herself. Tomorrow they'd show Coco how much fun it could be.

"It'll be better in the morning," Ollie said aloud. She licked crumbs off her fingers. "We're going to have so much fun."

"Yeah, I hope so," said Brian. He turned away from the window. "Group mission to brush teeth now? Or do you guys want to go out into that creepy, chilly hallway one at a time?"

Ollie and Coco shook their heads. Since October, none of them had liked being alone in the dark. It wasn't that they were *afraid*, exactly. But they had learned that bad things could happen to you. At night. Alone. In the dark. Not that there was anything bad in the hallway, Ollie reminded herself. But the three of them still stuck together. They'd been sticking together ever since they'd run the corn maze and escaped the scarecrows and met the smiling man.

Sometimes Ollie, Brian, and Coco argued. Sometimes they annoyed each other. But they stuck together. Even for little stuff. Like going to the bathroom down a spooky dark hallway. Coco was looking a lot happier. "Yep, let's go together," she said.

Ollie was so glad she had her friends.

———

That night, Ollie dreamed.

In her dream, someone was pulling at her sleeve.

"Go 'way," Ollie murmured. Even in her sleep, she wanted to sleep. But the tugging kept on.

A small voice whispered, "Please, can you help me?"

Dream-Ollie opened her eyes. She saw a girl about her own age standing by her bed, dressed in a long white nightgown. The girl's face was in shadow. The whole room was full of shadow and moonlight. "Can you help?" whispered the girl again in a thin, scratchy voice. "No one else wants to help."

Ollie realized that she was lying on one of a row of identical white beds. She couldn't see how long the row was. The end of it disappeared into the shadows. Ollie looked down at herself. She was wearing a white night-gown too.

She still couldn't see the face of the girl by her bed. Only the girl's hand gripping her sleeve. It was bony and gray; the nails were long and black. The fingertips were blackened too, like the girl had dipped her hands in ashes.

Ollie wrenched away, half falling over the other side of the bed.

"Please," the other girl's voice whined out of the darkness. "I'm looking for my bones. Can you help me find them?"

Bones? Ollie just wanted to get out of that room. She looked around for a door. There wasn't one. Just a lot of narrow white beds. The room was full of beds.

In each bed lay a girl. Their eyes were closed and frosted around with ice. Frozen shut? Their skin was all grayish. They looked like they'd frozen to death, stiff in their beds.

Ollie wanted to get away. But there was nowhere to go. Her heart beat faster and faster.

"I need my bones," whispered the girl again. "I can't get out of here without my bones."

Ollie tried to say something, but no sound came out.

Suddenly the other girl reached over and grabbed Ollie by the arm. Her hand was cold and skinny and strong. "*She's coming*," the girl hissed. "You have to help me. If she finds you here, she'll put you to bed. She'll put me to bed. And then she'll never let us leave again. Just like the others." She gestured at the sleeping girls all around them, with their eyes frozen shut. "You'll sleep here forever."

Footsteps sounded outside the room. The girl holding Ollie's arm cringed, but she didn't let go of Ollie's sleeve. "Good little girls don't try to leave," she muttered, almost to herself. "They stay here with Mother. Only bad little girls try to escape. But I'm a bad little girl. I don't want to stay here forever."

Her face was in the moonlight now. Unlike the other girls, her eyes were open, although ringed in frost. She looked like her eyes had frozen open, instead of shut. She didn't blink. Her wide eyes gave her an expression of startled horror.

Ollie's breath was shallow with terror. The quick, clacking footsteps outside were getting closer. "I don't know where your bones are," she managed.

The girl threw a terrified look at the door.

Then she bent forward and whispered in a totally

different voice, almost too low for Ollie to hear: "It doesn't matter. Don't listen to the voices."

"*What?*" Ollie's voice came out a thin, terrified whisper. "What voices?"

"The dead voices," said the girl. "All the dead voices." Her icy hand pinched Ollie's arm. "Stay out of closets. And don't look in the mirror."

Then the door to the room slammed open.

The girl screamed and threw herself backward, scrabbling away and disappearing into the shadows.

There was something in the doorway. Someone. It looked like a woman. Ollie couldn't see her face. Just that she was tall and wore a black dress. She advanced on Ollie and reached out a bony hand. "Awake?" she demanded.

Ollie didn't answer. She tried to get up and run, but she couldn't move.

"Bad little girl. I caught you red-handed! How dare you be awake! Lie down this instant! Get back in bed and *stay there*." The woman's bony hand descended, grabbing at her. Ollie finally got her breath and shrieked.

And came gasping awake, to find herself in the lower bunk of their room in Hemlock Lodge, in the pitch-black dark before dawn. Coco must have just gone to the bathroom. Ollie heard her climb the bunk ladder and settle again under the covers.

Ollie had to pee too. But she lay still in bed, trying to ignore it. She really didn't want to go out into the dark, freezing hallway.

She couldn't ignore it.

Annoyed, and still shaken from her nightmare, Ollie got up, shoved her feet into slippers, went out into the hall. It was inky dark, and freezing. She almost ran to the girls' bathroom. But she wasn't scared, she told herself. Just cold.

There was a light showing under the bathroom door. Ollie frowned. Hadn't they turned it off before going to bed? Despite herself, she was nervous. She scolded herself for being silly. Nightmares were just nightmares. Didn't she know that by now? She'd had enough of them.

Determinedly, Ollie stepped forward and opened the bathroom door just as one of the toilets flushed.

"Hello?" called Ollie. Her voice cracked a little. "Who's that?"

Coco stepped out of the stall, frowning.

"It's me," she said. "Who else would it be?"

Ollie stared. "But," she said, "I heard you get back in bed."

"Not yet," said Coco. "I had to pee. You probably heard the lodge creaking." Coco looked small and cold in her flannel pajamas. "This lodge creaks a lot. I've been hearing weird noises all night." She said it like she was trying to sound chill, but was a bit anxious herself.

Ollie nodded. "Yeah," she said, with feeling. "Although I was *sure* I heard . . . Wait for me to pee?" she asked.

"'Kay," said Coco, and Ollie was happy not to be alone.

She flushed the toilet, and together the girls went back to their room.

But Ollie stopped short in the doorway. She stared at Coco's bed.

It didn't look empty. For a second, she was sure she saw a small girl, ice in her wide-open eyes, sitting up, staring at her. Her lips moved, mouthed two words.

Don't listen.

With a gasp, Ollie leaped for the lamp, turned it on. There was no one there. Coco was peering at her worriedly. "What?" she said. "Did you see something?"

"Nothing," said Ollie. But her heart was racing. "Just imagining things."

———

It took Coco a long while to fall back asleep. She didn't like Hemlock Lodge. The old wood and plaster groaned and creaked. The wind whined under the eaves outside. Coco lay in her top bunk and peered into every shadow, half expecting one of them to move. What had made Ollie nervous? Just the dark? Bad dreams? Or something else?

32

But Coco must have fallen asleep at some point, because the next thing she remembered was hearing Ollie's gasp as she jerked awake below her. Pale morning light trickled between the curtains. Coco was happy to see the daylight. She dangled her head over the bunk and peered down at her friend. Ollie was as white as a piece of paper. Her curly brown hair stuck out every which way. "Ollie," said Coco. "You okay?"

Her friend was covered in sweat. "Nightmares," she said. She sat up and scrubbed a hand over her face. "A couple of *really* bad nightmares."

"I had one too," said Coco. "Yesterday in the car. You wanna talk about it?"

"Maybe," said Ollie. She rolled out of bed decisively, like she was eager to be out of it. "But I need hot chocolate first."

Hot chocolate sounded good to Coco too. "And a really, really big cinnamon roll." She started to untangle herself from her covers. "What did you dream?"

"I can't remember exactly." Ollie still looked shaken.

"Not scarecrows?"

"No," said Ollie. "Something about—about beds. And mirrors." She walked to the window and pulled back the curtain. Coco eyed the world outside, still in the safety of her top bunk. It looked *cold*. And white. And snowy. The snow was coming down as fast as it had the night before.

The wind hummed in the lines of the ski lift, like the whole mountain was a giant violin.

"No skiing unless the wind drops," Ollie said glumly, letting the curtain fall. "They won't be able to use the lifts while it's so windy. Let's go wake up Brian." For some reason, she seemed eager to be out of their room.

Brian was asleep, and *not* happy to be woken up. But the girls finally talked him out of his room and dragged him, wearing a gray hoodie, pajama pants, and a grumpy expression, down the hall and to the stairs. "There had *better* be hot chocolate in this place," he said as he followed them.

With only two windows at either end, the hall wasn't much brighter than it had been the night before. Ollie was still pale and tense too. Coco wondered what she'd been dreaming about.

In the lobby, the three of them found Sue Wilson behind the front desk, wearing a reindeer sweater and a huge smile. She hopped to her feet when she saw them. "Ah!" she said. "Early risers! And you five still the only guests here." Coco didn't think she was totally happy about that, despite the smile. "Breakfast?" she asked.

"Yes, please," said Brian immediately. "Is there hot chocolate?"

"You bet! Sam's cooking. He's a mean cook. We hired

a chef, but he couldn't make it. *None* of our staff could make it. We're *really* snowed in!"

Coco didn't think Mrs. Wilson was too happy about that either.

Ollie didn't seem to be listening. Which was strange for her, because she loved both hot chocolate and breakfast in general. She was frowning at a cluster of stuffed coyotes in a corner of the lobby. "Ollie, you coming?" called Brian, already heading for the dining room.

"Yeah," said Ollie. But she was still frowning.

"What's wrong?" Coco asked her.

"Nothing," said Ollie. "It's just I was sure I counted four coyotes last night. But it was dark."

"No, I thought there were four too," said Coco. She looked back at them. There were five. "Well, we probably just didn't see the fifth one, right?" she said.

"I guess," said Ollie. She shrugged and followed Brian into the dining room. Coco gave the coyotes a final glance. They were all showing big white teeth. Five doggy grins, like they were making fun of her. Had they looked like that last night?

Well, of course they had. How else would they have looked? Hurrying, Coco went after Ollie.

The dining room turned out to be right next to the lobby, and the two rooms were connected by a pair of archways. The fireplace that heated the lobby also heated the dining room. A fire was already roaring. The walls were clean white, freshly painted. A mirror hung on the wall opposite the fireplace, making the room seem even bigger than it was.

Coco's mom was sitting alone at a table beside the fireplace, sipping coffee and scrolling through the news on her phone. She'd plugged it into a nearby outlet. Coco was glad to see that. The outlets upstairs hadn't been working.

Coco's mom really didn't get cheerful until she'd had a second cup of coffee, but she looked up when they walked in and smiled at them all anyway. "You guys are up early," she said. "Did the wind wake you?"

"Nope," said Brian, still a little grumpy himself. "It was these two banging on the door. They tried to bribe me with hot chocolate."

"And it worked," Ollie commented.

Brian sighed. "Hot chocolate, my kryptonite," he said.

Ollie's dad popped out of the kitchen like a magic-trick rabbit. "Did I hear a call for hot chocolate? Coming right up!"

Ollie groaned and laughed and sank down into a chair next to Brian. "Dad's in the kitchen already," Ollie said.

"Why am I not surprised?" Coco laughed too, and took the chair on the other side of her mom. It was so like Ollie's dad to take over the lodge kitchen.

Coco's mom smiled again. She seemed, thought Coco, more cheerful than she usually was in the mornings. "Your dad does love cooking, doesn't he?" Coco's mom said to Ollie. "When I came down, he was already in the kitchen. Said he heard Sam Wilson swearing at the stove and smelled something burning. Of course, he had to jump in and lend a hand." She laughed and shook her head at the memory. Coco couldn't remember the last time she'd seen her mom laugh like that. She must like being on vacation, even if vacation so far was just sleeping in a weird ski lodge.

Mr. Adler popped out of the kitchen again, this time with a jug in one hand and a big platter of pancakes in the other. He marched over. "Breakfast coming up!" he announced in the booming voice of a circus ringmaster. They all giggled. Even Coco's mom.

"Come one, come all," continued Mr. Adler, sweeping over to the table. "And experience—PANCAKES. For Miss Olivia Adler, most favorite daughter, we have banana chocolate chip PANCAKES. For Miss Coco Zintner, favorite almost-daughter, blueberry! And for Mr. Brian Battersby, favorite almost-son and hometown hockey hero, buttermilk! And something left over for us, of course," he added, winking at Coco's mom. He plopped the pancake platter in the middle of the table, took the chair next to her, theatrically wiped his forehead, and helped himself to three pancakes. "Sam's bringing bacon and eggs," he added in a normal voice, waving his fork at the kitchen door. "Eat up!"

"And butter and maple syrup?" asked Brian hopefully, helping himself to a buttermilk pancake.

"And more coffee?" asked Coco's mom.

"It's like feeding an army, making breakfast for you four," said Mr. Adler. "But yes. What are pancakes without maple syrup? And I know you're a five-cups-a-morning kind of woman." He grinned at Coco's mom, took her hand, squeezed it briefly, and started cutting up his pancakes.

Ollie looked from her dad to Coco's mom with a strange expression. Coco was staring between the two of them herself. *Hand-holding? Where did that come from?*

Coco, wondering if she should say something, helped herself to a blueberry pancake and passed the platter. Ollie took a pancake, mouth shut tight, not meeting anyone's gaze.

Coco decided that she didn't dare say anything, if Ollie wasn't going to. She could ask her mom later.

Coco started on her pancake, and realized that she was happier than she'd been since they left East Evansburg. The smells of bacon, coffee, and pancakes filled the dining room. The fire was crackling, and she was nice and toasty. Mr. Adler had made them all laugh; her mom was smiling.

And Ollie's dad had held hands with her mom. Just for a second, but still. Coco was delighted. Ollie's dad was one of her favorite people.

Maybe, Coco thought, this trip to Mount Hemlock wasn't going to be so bad, after all.

But why wouldn't Ollie meet anyone's eyes?

"Better dig in to those pancakes," said Mr. Adler. "Or I'll start telling jokes again."

"Oh no," said Coco's mom, but she was still smiling. They all hastily began to eat their pancakes. Sam Wilson came out with a huge platter of bacon and scrambled eggs, and also a jug of golden maple syrup, some pats of butter, and a pot of coffee hanging dangerously from a pinkie. Ollie's dad raised a cheer at his appearance, and Mr. Wilson managed to set the food onto the table without spilling any of it.

"Whew," he said to Ollie's dad. "You're quite the chef, Roger. Glad you lent me a hand! Not to say I couldn't have done it all myself, but . . ."

"Have a bite, Sam," said Mr. Adler hospitably. "Don't be formal; there's only the seven of us here!"

"Well, don't mind if I do," said Mr. Wilson, and he sat.

"Guess there's not going to be any skiing today, huh?" Brian asked once he'd downed his first pancake. He peered out the window, a little glum. Coco felt sorry for him. She thought of how happily he'd talked of boots and skis and snow and trails on the drive up.

"Not today," said Mr. Adler. He sighed. "Too much wind. You guys probably heard the wind this morning. Absolutely shrieking. It woke Zelda and me up." (Zelda was Coco's mom.) "Besides, Sam says they've been having a lot of mechanical difficulties, isn't that right?"

Mr. Wilson gulped a bite of bacon, and said, "Never seen anything like it. The lift keeps breaking down. The generator's only putting out half—less—of the power it's supposed to, but I can't find anything wrong with it. It's just—not working."

Brian looked unhappy at the news. But Coco's heart leaped at the words *not today*.

No slippery cold mountain, she thought. *Great. We can stay here and play chess. Or Scrabble. We can draw. Read.*

Ollie was good at chess too. Coco practiced more, but Ollie was smart: the best at math in the entire middle school, and her mom had taught her to play chess when she was little. Brian *could* play chess, though he didn't love it. He was a mean hand at Scrabble. Coco thought contentedly of spending a cozy day by the fire playing board games with her friends.

"We're just going to have to entertain ourselves," said Mr. Adler, echoing Coco's thought.

But Brian kept on staring sadly out the big window of the dining room. Coco felt a little guilty for being so happy that they couldn't ski. Ollie looked like she was hardly listening to what people were saying. She was watching her dad and Coco's mom.

Was Ollie *upset* about the hand-holding? Coco wondered.

"Maybe we can raid the kitchen and bake cookies," Mr. Adler suggested. "I'll teach you all to knit. Got any board games, Sam?"

"A couple," said Mr. Wilson. "I'll go dig them out after breakfast."

"Maybe at least we can go sledding," said Brian, still staring out into the white world. "It doesn't matter if it's windy for that."

"Maybe," said Mr. Adler doubtfully. "It's really coming down, though."

Coco poured herself more hot chocolate.

Suddenly Brian said, "Hey, guys. Look. Who's that?"

Everyone turned to look. It was a car. A black car, covered in snow, making its creeping way across the parking lot.

"Huh," said Coco. "Someone made it through the storm."

"I'm impressed that anything besides a plow truck

could get up here," said Coco's mom. They had all stopped eating their pancakes to watch.

The black car, skidding, finally made it across the parking lot and quivered to a halt beside the white lump that was all that could be seen of Susie the Subaru. The driver got out. He was wearing a black ski jacket.

They waited. The next second, there was the sound of the big front doors opening, and a shriek of wind from outside. Over the wind came the sound of Mrs. Wilson saying hello in her breathless voice.

An unfamiliar voice answered; the door slammed shut.

Mrs. Wilson said something else. The visitor laughed. Then Mrs. Wilson appeared in the dining room, the car's driver trailing her.

As he came in, he briskly peeled off layers, shedding melting snowflakes. He wasn't that tall: shorter than Ollie's dad. He had freckles across his nose and a bony, serious sort of face, with black-rimmed glasses. He looked a little like their history teacher at school, Coco thought. As he walked into the dining room, he smiled at them and said, "Hello, all. So glad I made it. Do you mind if I sit down?"

The stranger didn't wait for anyone to nod, but dropped at once into the seat next to Mr. Wilson. "Drove all night," he said. "What a storm! I wasn't sure I'd make it. I thought they'd be fishing me out of the river this spring, for sure. Is that coffee?" He didn't wait for an answer. He seized a clean mug, poured himself a cup, and gulped.

Mrs. Wilson, Coco saw, just seemed confused. Maybe they were all a little confused by the sudden appearance of this stranger. Mrs. Wilson said, "I'm sorry, what was your name again? If I could just find you on the original guest list . . ."

"Oh!" said the man. "I'm not on it. Name's Don Voland. I'm a reporter. On magazine assignment. Pleased to meet you." He reached around the table, shook everyone's hands, winked at the kids. His eyes were two different colors, Coco was startled to see. One green, the other dark. The two-colored eyes stood out strangely against his freckles.

Mrs. Wilson and Coco's mom both suddenly looked really happy. "Oh!" said Mrs. Wilson. "A *journalist*! Here to report on our ski mountain? How lovely. Sam and I would be happy to answer any questions." She sat down, folded her hands, and gave Don Voland a huge smile.

Coco's mom said, "Which magazine? I'm a journalist myself."

Mr. Voland looked slightly apologetic. He scratched the back of his neck. Coco noticed that, oddly, his first two fingers were exactly the same length. "Well," he said, "it's a magazine called *Light*, and I don't really write about skiing, sorry, ma'am." He bobbed his head. "I write about ghosts."

He drank more coffee. Everyone at the table stared at him.

Mrs. Wilson looked instantly frosty. "What do you mean, ghosts?"

Mr. Voland had pulled a plate over without even asking and was helping himself to the pancakes. Mr. Wilson looked like he wanted to tell Mr. Voland that pancakes were for guests only, sorry. But even though he opened his mouth, he shut it without saying anything.

Mr. Voland said, pouring maple syrup, "Yes, I write about ghosts. Hauntings, odd occurrences, and things that cannot be explained. Ghosts!" He took a bite, chewed his pancake. "These are great."

"My dad made them," put in Ollie.

"Compliments to the chef," said Mr. Voland to Mr. Adler. He was looking around the dining room with interest, still chewing.

Ollie watched Mr. Voland warily. Brian did too. Coco supposed she looked uneasy herself. The three of them had seen ghosts. *And* things they could not explain. In October. Behind the mist. Would Mr. Voland know about those things? Coco wondered.

"And what makes you think that Hemlock Lodge—" started Mrs. Wilson.

Mr. Voland said, still smiling, "Well, there were all

those stories about this place. While it was shut up. Didn't you know? I'm sure someone mentioned it when you bought the building. The orphanage didn't have the best reputation." He ate more pancake.

Coco thought of a dark figure on the road, a shadow in an empty hall.

Across the table, Ollie bit her lip. "Old orphanage?" she blurted out. "I thought this used to be a school."

"It was," broke in Mr. Wilson. "A fine institution! I don't know what you are implying . . . what was your name again?"

"Don will do." Mr. Voland leaned back, cradling his mug of coffee. "And to answer your question," he added. "It was a school *and* an orphanage. Apparently it wasn't all sunshine and roses. Rumors went around that children were being locked in closets and things. No one investigated at the time, though—people didn't really care about orphans. And after the orphanage was closed, people started seeing strange lights in the windows. Once the police were called because someone heard screaming inside the building. But they never found anyone. Stories about this place started to go up and down the valley. The most common was the story of a little girl named Gretel and a woman called Mother Hemlock. Ever heard the story?"

They shook their heads. Mr. Wilson was red with annoyance; Mrs. Wilson still looked frosty. Ollie looked like she was listening hard.

"Well, Gretel was an orphan at the school, apparently," said Mr. Voland. "She wasn't a very good student; she liked to go poking around, instead of paying attention at her lessons. Sometimes she'd even get up at night and wander the halls. Some of the stories say she sleepwalked. Others that she was just curious." He paused to eat some bacon, then went on. "Mother Hemlock was a teacher who lived at the orphanage. She was quite strict. She got more and more angry each time she found Gretel in the hall when she ought to have been asleep, or in class. Finally, one day, she'd had enough. She caught Gretel wandering about, hauled her upstairs, and locked the girl in a closet. 'I'll teach you to go disappearing!' she said. 'Sit there and see what happens to bad girls!' She left. Gretel was afraid of the dark. She screamed and screamed, but no one came. That night, when Mother Hemlock came to let her out, she found that the little girl had died of fright."

Ollie's eyes were huge. "A closet?" she asked unexpectedly.

Mr. Voland said, "Well, yes, I believe that is the story." He went on:

"They say that Gretel has haunted the lodge ever since.

People hear her rattling closet doors, skipping and whistling in the hallways. Mother Hemlock, the legend says, threw herself out the attic window in remorse. Now she haunts the building too. Some stories say she collects the souls of all the little girls who ever died in the orphanage. Others say she is eternally trying to keep Gretel's ghost from running away again. And Gretel is eternally trying to escape."

No one said anything. There was an uneasy silence. Coco thought suddenly of her dream of a long corridor, and a little dead girl standing in the moonlight.

Mr. Voland sat back, smiled, and shrugged. He took a sip of coffee. "At least," he said, "that's the story."

Mr. Wilson, Coco noticed, was still bright red with annoyance. "I'm sorry," he said. "You can't just come and tell these terrible—"

At the same time, Ollie blurted out, "What do they look like?"

Mr. Voland said, frowning, "What do who look like?"

"The ghosts!" said Ollie. "Gretel and—and Mother Hemlock. What do they look like?"

Mr. Voland peered at Ollie over the tops of his glasses. He seemed puzzled by her question. "I don't know," he said. "The stories talk more about *hearing* them than seeing them." His eyes narrowed. "Why do you ask?"

Why *had* Ollie asked? Coco wondered. Her mom and Ollie's dad were wearing expressions of tolerant amusement. Neither of them, Coco knew, believed in ghosts.

"No reason," said Ollie, too quickly. Coco wondered if Ollie had seen anything strange in the lodge. Or if Brian had. The three of them needed to talk *soon*, she decided.

Another little silence went around the table. The wind groaned outside.

"Of course," Mr. Voland went on, with an apologetic nod at Mrs. Wilson, "I am sorry to disturb your breakfast with ghost stories. But when I heard that the old building was open again, free to all, this time as a ski lodge, I decided it was the perfect time to look into it. Coming to a lovely ski lodge sounded much better than breaking into an abandoned orphanage. Food's much better." He ate some more eggs, happily.

At the words *breaking into*, Mr. Wilson started looking irritated all over again.

"And I am so delighted to be here and so impressed with what you've done with the place, ma'am," Mr. Voland finished. He swallowed more coffee.

Mrs. Wilson said coldly, "Thank you. And I want to tell you at the outset that all this is quite ridiculous. The building was an orphanage and is now a ski lodge. I don't know what you're hoping to find."

"Me neither," said Mr. Voland comfortably. "Never know until you look."

Coco had a sudden, clear memory of a girl's dry, dead voice saying, *I'm looking for my bones.* Even though the fire was burning brightly, the dining room suddenly felt cold. Coco wished Mr. Voland hadn't come. She glanced at the window. The snow was coming down harder and faster than ever. Susie the Subaru was totally buried.

"Don't you worry, ma'am," said Mr. Voland reassuringly to Mrs. Wilson. "A good ghost story is great for business, true or no."

Just then, all the lights in the dining room flickered. Coco looked up. A log crumbled in the fireplace with a shower of sparks, and somewhere out of sight, someone whistled.

"What was that?" Ollie asked. "I thought we were the only people here."

"Oh!" said Mrs. Wilson firmly. "Just the generators acting up again. And that was my clock chiming—it does birdcalls at each hour, isn't that nice?"

Coco didn't think it was that nice at all. The chiming clock had sounded just like a little girl might sound, whistling in the corridors. Ollie, Brian, and Coco all looked at one another, and Coco saw the same thought echoed on all their faces.

"Now," Mrs. Wilson was saying briskly, "enough ghost stories. Sam and I will just clear away the empty dishes, and you all can have more hot drinks."

But right at that moment, all the lights in the dining room flickered again and went out. Then, with a hiss like a basket of snakes, a huge mass of snow fell straight down the chimney and smothered the fire.

3

COCO STARED AT the dead fire. Mr. Voland stopped eating, his fork halfway to his mouth. Ollie had shot to her feet.

"Now, now," said Mrs. Wilson at once. "No need for alarm."

Ollie slowly sank back down.

Mrs. Wilson got up. "Nothing to worry about," she said. "Snow down the chimney! I'll get it cleared out. We've had *such* a run of bad luck."

Mrs. Wilson hurried away. Coco thought she looked glad to get away from Mr. Voland.

Sam Wilson said, standing, "I'd better help her. Thanks for helping out in the kitchen this morning, Roger." He shook Mr. Adler's hand. "Zelda," he said, nodding at Coco's mom. He didn't say anything to Mr. Voland.

"Don't mention it, Sam," said Ollie's dad. He took his last drink of coffee.

Mr. Voland lifted his head and frowned. "Hear that?" he said.

"No," said Ollie's dad. "What?"

"Well, it's more a nothing than a something," Mr. Voland replied. "Sounds like the generator's out. Hope the heat is gas powered. Otherwise we're going to be pretty chilly tonight."

Coco hoped so too. The lodge was chilly enough *with* the heat going.

"The heat is gas powered," said Ollie's dad. "And I'm sure we'll have the generators going soon. No worries there. I think I'll go help Sam with the dishes. Nice to meet you, Don. Kids, finish your pancakes." He snagged the last piece of bacon and headed in the direction of the kitchen, humming.

Just like that, breakfast had mostly broken up.

"I am sure you have some good stories from ghost hunting," Coco's mom said to Mr. Voland, pouring herself more coffee. She said it politely, but she seemed disappointed with him anyway. Coco's mom might have been excited to talk to a real journalist, but some ghost hunter didn't count.

"I sure do," said Mr. Voland with enthusiasm. "And maybe after today I'll have another." He gave the dining hall an eager look. Coco didn't know what he was so happy about. The snow piling up outside the windows made the dining room seem gray and lonely.

Coco's mom looked skeptical. "Maybe."

Mr. Voland grinned at her. "Come on now," he said. "What better thing to do in an old lodge while the power is out than go looking for ghosts?"

"Bake cookies?" suggested Coco's mom at once. But she was smiling too. Mr. Voland was strange, but his eagerness was contagious. "I'd rather finish the day with oatmeal cookies than any number of ghosts."

Coco agreed. She was really hoping that today *didn't* become a good ghost-hunting story for Mr. Voland.

"Well, there may be time for both," said Mr. Voland, and smacked his lips. "The supernatural goes well with peanut butter cookies!"

Coco's mother snorted. "If you say so. Roger makes great cookies," she said. "Maybe we can convince him later. In the meantime, I think I'll help Sue with the fireplace. If you're okay here, hon?" The last sentence was to Coco.

"Fine," said Coco, a little embarrassed to be treated like a kid in front of her friends.

Coco's mom stood up and cracked her neck. The fireplace was a mess of ash and water, and Mrs. Wilson was shoveling it out, swearing under her breath. "Good luck with your ghost hunting, Don," said Coco's mom. "Got an extra shovel, Sue?" She headed over to the fireplace.

Then it was just the four of them at the table. Ollie, Brian, and Coco were getting full; they picked at their pancakes. Mr. Voland ate some more eggs, looking thoughtful. Coco was just about to suggest that she, Ollie, and Brian sneak off for a conference, when Mr. Voland turned abruptly to Ollie. "Why did you ask me what the ghosts *looked* like?" he asked. "It was an odd question."

Ollie hesitated. Then she asked a question in return. "Mr. Voland," she said, "have you ever seen a ghost?"

"I have," said Mr. Voland. "Have you?"

Ollie, frowning, gave a small nod. Mr. Voland's expression sharpened. "What's your name?"

"Ollie," said Ollie. "This is Brian, and that's Coco."

"Pleased to meet you all," he said. His two-colored eyes seemed to stare straight through them.

Coco asked, "Were you scared? When you saw a ghost?"

"I was," said Mr. Voland immediately. His lips went thin, as though he was remembering something unpleasant. But then he shrugged, dabbed his mouth with a napkin, and said, "It was a long time ago." His eyes brightened. "Well, it seems you three are old hands at this ghost business. Do you want to explore the lodge with me this morning?"

Why hadn't he asked them *where* they'd seen ghosts? Coco wondered. She did *not* want to explore the lodge. She was already worried about strange dreams, and strange figures in the shadows. She didn't want to add anything else to the mix. She opened her mouth to say so.

But Ollie spoke first. "I'd like that," she said.

"How lovely!" said Mr. Voland. He leaped to his feet.

Ollie hopped up too. "Let's start now," she said determinedly.

Brian frowned at Ollie, then shrugged and nodded agreement.

Coco shut her mouth again, wilting. Her friends already knew Coco had been scared about skiing. Now was she going to be scared about this too? What would they both think? So, Coco just nodded too.

But she almost wanted to cry, thinking of the warm fireplace, her sketchbook, and her chessboard. Why did her friends want to go looking for scary stuff?

"Mr. Voland," Ollie said, her expression still strangely eager, "have you ever *talked* to a ghost?"

Mr. Voland had produced a thermos from his jacket pocket; he was pouring the rest of the coffee into it. "Yes," said Mr. Voland, not looking up. "There are tools for that. Talking to ghosts is much more common than seeing them, actually."

"How do you talk to ghosts?" Ollie asked. She sounded

like she was just asking a casual question. But as she talked, Ollie glanced down, just once, at the watch on her wrist.

Coco saw her do it. Instantly she understood why her friend was suddenly so eager to go ghost hunting.

Ollie's watch wasn't an ordinary watch. It looked ordinary: just a big digital watch with a compass. But Ollie's mother had been wearing that watch when she died in a plane crash the year before. Its face was cracked; its compass didn't point north.

However, that October, when Ollie, Brian, and Coco had been in terrible danger, Ollie's mother had talked to her through words on the watch face. Had helped them. Guided them. Saved them. *Of course* Ollie would grab the chance to learn more about ghosts, Coco realized. She wanted to know more about how her watch worked.

Mr. Adler popped back in from the kitchen. A few yards away, Mrs. Wilson and Coco's mom were attacking the fireplace with mops and shovels and buckets. "Zelda," he called, "looks like the dishes are under control. I was thinking maybe we could go out and see what went wrong with the generators? If you know anything about generators, because I sure don't."

Coco's mom sat back on her heels, a smudge of ash on one cheek. "As a matter of fact, I do," she said. "Surprised? Coco's grandpa was an electrician. Where's the generator shed? Let me get my jacket."

She turned to Ollie, Brian, and Coco and gave them a stern look. "You three need to stay *inside* today. Don't make us go looking for you. It's snowing a whiteout out there. Right, sweetie?" she added to Coco.

Coco nodded. Her mom pulled her in for an un-expected hug. "Be good," she said. "I love you."

Coco straightened up just in time to see Ollie turn away, her teeth sunk into her lower lip.

Ollie was thinking of her own mom, Coco thought. She ached for her friend. Ollie hated getting sympathy from anyone, but Coco couldn't help trying. "Ollie—" she started, but Ollie wasn't listening.

"What stuff do we need?" Ollie asked Mr. Voland briskly.

Mr. Adler and Coco's mom were heading out of the room in search of jackets and boots. Mr. Voland put the lid on his thermos, took a final pancake, rolled it up around some egg, like a burrito, wrapped it in a napkin, and tucked it into a pocket. "You just need your wits about you," he told them. "A notebook and a pencil to write down any impressions. And maybe a flashlight."

"We'll go up to our rooms right now to get our stuff," said Ollie. "We'll meet you in the lobby." Without another word, she bolted for the stairs, running ahead of Coco and Brian. She disappeared into the shadows of the second floor. Coco and Brian followed her.

Mr. Voland stayed in the lobby.

"Guess we're going to look for ghosts," said Coco unhappily.

"It's not my first choice either, Tiny," said Brian.

Coco looked at him in surprise. At breakfast, Brian had seemed happy to go ghost hunting. "Ollie's upset," he added. "You noticed, right? Probably about your mom and her dad holding hands." Brian said it like it was the most obvious thing in the world. Maybe it was, to him. People all said hockey was Brian's superpower, but Coco thought his superpower was noticing things. "And *Ollie's* mom might be a ghost. Therefore—ghost hunting. We can't just let her go looking for ghosts all upset and by herself."

"No," Coco agreed. "We can't. But, I mean, we don't *know* if her dad and my mom like each other."

Brian gave her a skeptical look.

Coco bit her lip. She was afraid to believe it because she wanted it to be true so badly. She wanted to move into the Egg with her mom and live with Ollie and Ollie's dad. She wanted Ollie to be her actual sister, not just her friend. But Ollie— "Ollie doesn't want *my* mom," said Coco sadly. "She wants her own mom back."

"Obviously," said Brian. "Wouldn't you?"

Coco didn't answer that. Instead she said, "It's just that—I'm still not sure that ghost hunting is a good idea." Suddenly Coco's worries came pouring out in a rush. "Last night, on the road, I think I might have seen a ghost. Really. I saw someone in a blue ski jacket who vanished. And then . . ." Coco swallowed. "I saw the shadow of a person in the second-floor hall. But there wasn't anyone there. Just the shadow. And Ollie had nightmares all night. She hasn't said what about, but she looked scared when she woke up this morning. And the generators aren't working. And we can't leave until the storm stops. Maybe this place really is haunted. Brian, do you really *want* to meet another ghost? Be stuck here in a snowstorm with ghosts?"

Brian had stopped dead at the foot of the stairs. "Seriously?" said Brian. "You've been actually seeing *ghosts*? And you didn't tell me?"

"I didn't know what I was seeing! You didn't believe me last night on the road. And this morning, we were kind of distracted by pancakes and a random guy showing up and our parents *holding hands*," retorted Coco.

"Yeah," said Brian. "Sorry about last night. I did kind of think you were dreaming."

"And now?" said Coco.

"I believe you," said Brian. He paused, thinking. "The three of us clearly need to talk ASAP."

"Yeah," said Coco. "And we need to stick together. Like always, right? We'll stick together, and we'll be fine."

Brian grinned. "As always, Tiny," he said, making Coco want to smile and stomp on his foot at the same time.

"Don't call me Tiny," she said for about the thousandth time. "We'd better go find Ollie."

They started up the stairs. But with his foot on the second step, Brian paused, frowning, and turned back. "Wasn't the bear on its hind legs before?" he asked.

Coco turned. The stuffed bear was on all fours, its head twisted back over its shoulder, like it was looking at them. She frowned. "I think it was," she said. "I can't really remember now."

"Never mind," said Brian. They got to the top of the stairs. The hallway was shadowy. The wall lamps were off. There was only the light coming from the windows on each end. Coco couldn't see Ollie. She must already be in their room.

Halfway down the hall, Brian slowed. Stopped. "Tiny," he said, "do you—hear something?"

Coco stopped, listened.

"No—" she began.

"*Listen,*" said Brian.

And then she heard it. A very soft rattle.

"Maybe it's Ollie," said Coco, but she realized she was whispering.

"Maybe—" said Brian, and then there was a bang, right next to them, like someone had slammed a fist against the wall. They both jumped.

Now all was silent. They listened. Nothing. "Where'd

it come from?" Coco asked, hearing her voice go thin with anxiety.

"I don't know—" Brian began.

Another rattle. Coco turned.

"There?" asked Brian. He pointed. To their right was a door labeled UTILITY CLOSET.

"Who would be in—?" Coco broke off. The door was shaking on its hinges, knob going back and forth, like someone inside was trying to turn it. But it was locked. Who would be in there?

"Ollie?" called Brian. "Ollie, that's not funny."

No answer. The door shook again.

Brian said, staring at the door, "Do you think—"

"I don't know," said Coco. "I thought I heard—*listen*."

Brian shushed. Silence fell once more in the hall. The door was still.

And then Coco heard a voice.

A very small, very scratchy voice whispered, from behind the closet door, "Is anyone there?"

They both froze.

"Can I come out?" said the voice. "I'm scared." The door handle jerked up and down.

"But," said Brian, "if that's not Ollie, then *who is talking*?"

Coco didn't say anything. Her mouth and throat had gone dry.

61

The tiny trembling voice only went on, "I'll be goodest. I promise. I *promise!*" The door rattled harder than ever. "Let me out! *Let me out!*"

Coco and Brian looked at each other. "Was there someone else in the lodge? That we didn't know about?" Coco asked. But she knew there hadn't been.

"No," whispered Brian.

"Should we open the door?"

"Definitely not."

"Whoever it is, they're *scared*," said Coco.

The closet door rattled again.

Coco's hand darted out, hesitated on the handle. "Coco!" cried Brian.

But before she could lose her nerve, Coco wrenched the knob and threw open the door. It wasn't locked. They both stumbled back. She heard Brian's quick, frightened breath.

They both stared into the closet. But there was nothing in there at all.

4

OLLIE WAS IN the bunk room, pulling on an extra sweat-shirt. The bunk room had been warm the night before, but now it was chilly. The whole lodge seemed to be getting colder, Ollie thought. As though the storm outside was pressing inward, creeping in through cracks.

Ollie's insides were cold too, but it had nothing to do with the storm. She was sad. She was confused.

She'd forgotten how her dad had been before the plane crash. She'd forgotten how silly he could be, how fun. It was more than just bad jokes. It was the way he used to laugh, how things like banana pancakes for breakfast could make him so happy. She'd forgotten all that.

But that morning, her dad had been his old self. He'd been cooking, and laughing, and announcing his pancakes like a circus ringmaster. He'd plunked down the pancakes, winked at Coco's mom, and held her hand. Did he—*like* Coco's mom? Ollie wasn't sure what to think about that. Maybe she was imagining things. Coco's mom wasn't that special! Ollie's mom had been special. The most special person who ever lived.

But Ollie's mom was gone. And now Ollie didn't know how she should feel.

She thought about Coco. Ollie loved Coco. Coco was like her sister. She would *love* for Coco to be her real sister. That seemed like a big step, though. And Ollie didn't want another mother. Absolutely not!

But maybe she was wrong, Ollie thought. Imagining things. What if she went down and told her dad what she was feeling, and he had no idea what she was talking about? She'd be so embarrassed. Maybe none of this was real, and she was anxious over nothing.

More than anything, Ollie wanted to talk to her own mom. She wondered if Mr. Voland knew how. She hoped he did. She was going to help him explore the lodge, talk to him, and when the time was right, she was going to ask him. Casually. About how you talked to ghosts.

At that moment, Ollie's watch beeped.

She froze.

Ollie's watch hadn't changed or made a sound since those dangerous days when Ollie and her friends escaped the corn maze. But now the watch was beeping.

Ollie looked down at it.

Ever since October, there had been a single word, unchanged, on the digital display. LOVE, her watch had said. It was her mother's final message, sent after Ollie and her friends were safe.

But now the word was gone from the display, as though it had sunk in a gray sea. In its place, a word was struggling to get out. Letters and numbers writhed across the screen. But they were a blur. An *S*? *H*? Ollie couldn't read them.

"Mom?" she whispered. She looked around the room, but of course she was alone. Her heart was beating very fast. "Mom—are you there?" Maybe her mom was there to give her answers after all. If only Ollie could read . . . "What is it?"

For the briefest instant, a new word appeared on the watch face, then vanished as fast as it had come. The beeping stopped.

Ollie shook the watch. Tapped it. Nothing.

The word LOVE did not come back. Neither did the other word. The new word, which Ollie had barely glimpsed.

BEWARE.

Ollie was suddenly aware of the utter stillness of the room. The only sound was the moan of the wind outside. Where were Brian and Coco?

Her watch remained blank.

She waited. Nothing happened. Ollie started to shake. She couldn't stand still.

She bolted out the door and down the stairs.

Beware what?

Her hand closed tight around the empty watch face.

There was no sign of Brian or Coco in the lobby. Mr. Voland was leaning on the wall by the double-sided fireplace, talking to Mrs. Wilson. She was still digging in the ashes. Her hands were sooty to the elbows, and the corners of her mouth turned down. There was water everywhere from melted snow, but no fire. The lights were still out.

Ollie stepped around the bearskin rug, spared a frown at the bear in the corner. Hadn't it been on its hind legs before? Maybe Mr. Wilson had a lot of differently posed animals that he switched in and out?

"Oh," Mrs. Wilson was saying to Mr. Voland, in the tone of someone who was being polite but really just wanted to get on with work. "I didn't realize that a haunted lodge could be a tourist attraction."

Mr. Voland laughed his big, warm laugh. "It certainly can," he said cheerfully. "Give your lodge a haunted reputation, invent some bloodcurdling stories for a few of the rooms, and people will flock—absolutely flock—to stay here."

"Wish they would flock today," said Mrs. Wilson

sourly, and then she caught sight of Ollie. "Hello, dear!" she called. "Enjoying yourself?"

"Doing just fine, Mrs. Wilson," Ollie said. Still out of breath from running, she turned to Mr. Voland. "Could I talk to you a second, please?" she said.

Mr. Voland raised both eyebrows. "Ollie, wasn't it? Certainly." He walked over to a pair of cowskin chairs on the other side of the lobby and sat down on one. Ollie followed and took the other. She was almost quivering with impatience. The BEWARE on her mother's watch seemed to be burned onto the backs of her eyelids. She was barely sitting down before she blurted out, "If a ghost wanted to talk to *you*, how would you talk back? Can you tell me?"

Mr. Voland looked surprised. He thought a moment. Then he said, "I'll tell you what I know." He was watching her narrowly. "If you'll tell me why you're so interested. If it's just for fun, I'm afraid that talking to ghosts is not something one does for fun."

"It's not for fun!" Ollie burst out, more sharply than she'd meant. But Mr. Voland didn't look annoyed. He just waited.

Ollie didn't know what to say. Her watch was her precious secret, even now, when it had gone blank and she was afraid something had happened to it.

67

"I *know* ghosts are real," Ollie said carefully. "You say you've seen them. Me 'n' Brian 'n' Coco have all seen them too. So I want to know how you talk to them. That's all."

Mr. Voland said mildly, "I can't help you unless you tell me everything, Ollie."

She glared. He raised his eyebrows, still waiting.

Hesitating, Ollie began again, "My mom died. In a plane crash."

She darted a glance up at his face. More than anything, Ollie hated sympathy face: that look of solemn pity she got from grown-ups who knew she'd lost her mom. But Mr. Voland looked completely unmoved, except for mild interest. "I am so sorry," he said. "I assume you are hoping to talk to your lost mother, then? You do realize that talking to her won't bring her back."

"I *know* that," said Ollie, between clenched teeth. "That's not what I—"

"Talking to her," Mr. Voland went on relentlessly, "won't make you any less jealous of your friend, whose mother is there to worry about her and make her sandwiches, who will always love her more than you. So what do you hope to gain?"

Ollie gaped. "*Jealous?* Of my friend? You mean Coco? But I—I would never be. That's not why I wanted . . ." She trailed off, staring at him.

"No?" said Don. He leaned forward, elbows on knees, the two-colored eyes intent. "Then start from the beginning and tell me the truth, Ollie."

Ollie bit her lip and glared. She didn't want to tell him about her watch. She didn't want to tell him *anything* now. What right did he have to say something like that? She wasn't *jealous* of Coco. She *loved* Coco. Even if Coco could be annoying and sometimes Coco did complain about her mom, and hug her mom, never thinking about how it would make Ollie feel . . .

"I—" Ollie began. But she was cut off by her watch, which started beeping again, loudly and furiously. Ollie looked down. Still blank.

Then she heard a sudden thunder of footsteps down the stairs. Ollie looked up. Brian and Coco came sprinting into the lobby, and both of them were pale and stammering.

Mr. Voland looked once, narrow-eyed, from Ollie's still-beeping watch to Brian's and Coco's frightened faces. But he didn't say anything about the watch. Instead he turned to Ollie's friends. "Has something happened?"

They launched into speech together. He raised a hand. "One at a time, please."

Taking turns, Brian and Coco blurted out a strange story about a rattling closet and a voice inside, begging.

"But when we opened it," Coco finished breathlessly, "no one was there."

Ollie frowned, listening. The word *closet* rang a bell. Something she'd dreamed?

"Well," Don said, "it seems that the simplest course will be to investigate this closet." He looked excited. "The sooner the better." He took off up the stairs at once. Brian and Coco, after a brief hesitation, tagged along at his heels, looking anxious, leaving Ollie behind.

Ollie's watch had stopped beeping, but the face was still blank.

"What are you trying to tell me?" Ollie whispered.

No answer. Ollie clenched her fists and hurried after Brian and Coco. She couldn't let anything happen to her friends. She *had* to find a way to talk to her mom!

She caught the others at the top of the stairs. Ollie gave the rest of the hallway a suspicious look, but there was no one there except for them.

"Is this the closet?" Mr. Voland was asking Brian and Coco.

"That one," said Brian, pointing. It was a plain white door with a sign that said UTILITY CLOSET. He and Coco were both looking at that ordinary closet door like it contained snakes.

"Excellent," said Don, rubbing his hands together.

"Well, first let us see if the situation repeats itself. A knocking, was it? Hush, let us listen."

They all fell silent. Ollie glanced again at the empty gray screen of her watch. The sight made her feel cold and scared, as though a steadying hand had gone.

Silence lay thick in that lodge. But it wasn't, Ollie thought, an empty silence. It felt heavy now. Aware. Like someone was watching them, just around the corner. The back of her neck prickled. She looked up and down the hallway. Still no one but them.

"Nothing so far," said Don, after they'd listened in silence for a few minutes. His eyes were bright and eager. "Now we'll see what's inside the closet."

When he reached out and opened the door, Brian and Coco took a step back.

But the closet was empty. Just some brooms, a few spray bottles.

"Nothing," said Ollie.

"No—wait," said Brian. "What's that?" He pulled out his phone and shined the light into the closet. Ollie, standing behind him, saw a curving line carved raggedly into the back wall, half concealed by the mops. Above the line were two vertical slashes. Together they made . . .

"It's a face," said Coco, whispering. "It's sort of like a smiley face."

"Old graffiti," said Don. "Not everything has to do with ghosts. Even the sturdiest ghost isn't going to go carving things into walls."

"Still it's weird, though," said Brian. He started to edge into the closet, pushing the mops to one side.

A whole sentence flashed through Ollie's brain. *Stay out of closets.* Without thinking, she jumped forward, grabbed Brian by the hoodie, and hauled him back.

"Hey," she said. "It might not be safe."

"It's just a closet," said Brian.

Behind them, Coco suddenly cried out in a trembling voice, "Look! *Look!*"

They all whirled around. A tall black shape stood at the end of the hallway.

Ollie recognized it. She'd seen it in a dream, whispering *bad* in the dark. It wore a black dress that swept the carpet, and they couldn't see its face at all, because the dim light shone behind, casting its shadow long over the floor.

It pointed at them. It smiled, a vast, bony smile. They shuddered.

And then it turned and vanished, as quickly as it had come.

They all stared in stunned silence.

"I think," said Coco in a very small voice, "that I don't want to look for ghosts anymore."

"What *was* that?" demanded Brian.

"Mother Hemlock, maybe," said Mr. Voland, looking positively delighted. "Unless we are all hallucinating. Shall we continue?" He was staring eagerly down the hallway, like a dog pointing after a bird. "Make sure you write down your impressions for future comparison."

"Absolutely not," said Coco, with surprising force. She didn't move. "I want to go back to the lobby."

"Me too," said Ollie, just as strongly. "There's something wrong."

5

"NOW," SAID MR. VOLAND. He looked annoyed. "I am sorry that the first appearance of an unearthly being has alarmed you, but—"

"But, nothing," said Ollie firmly. "That was scary and it might be dangerous. We're going back to the lobby."

"Ghosts, while sometimes sinister, are rarely dangerous," said Mr. Voland. "What makes you think that one was?"

Ollie glanced down at her watch. Still blank. "Just a hunch," she said.

Mr. Voland looked like he didn't believe her. But without letting him say anything else, Ollie turned and headed down the stairs. Her friends followed. "Suit yourselves," said Mr. Voland, shrugging, and took off by himself down the hallway. Ollie glanced back just in time to see him disappearing into the dimness after the gaunt, grinning ghost. She shivered.

Ollie, Brian, and Coco hurried down the stairs. Brian looked surprised that Ollie had changed her mind. Coco just seemed happy that Ollie had backed her up. "You know," said Brian as they walked, "that was—freaky, but we did kind of sign up for ghost hunting. Not that I'm complaining, but what made you change your mind, Owl?"

Coco and Brian were the only two people in the whole world who knew what Ollie's watch could do. In a hurried whisper, Ollie told them about BEWARE. "I thought we just needed to be extra careful," Ollie explained. "Until we know *why* it said that." She added, hesitating, "And—that ghost in the hallway—I recognized her. I saw her in my nightmare last night." She shot another glance back up the dim stairwell. "I figured that can't be a good sign."

"You *dreamed* about who—Mother Hemlock?" Brian demanded. "If that's who she was?"

"I think so," said Ollie. "But last night, I didn't even know she *existed*."

Coco said suddenly, "I had a nightmare on the road last night. About a little girl who kept saying she'd lost her bones. There was a scarecrow in it too."

"There was a girl in my dream too!" exclaimed Ollie. "*She* said she'd lost her bones. And she said *don't listen*."

"Don't listen to what?" asked Coco.

"To the dead voices," said Ollie. Her lips and hands felt suddenly cold. "Don't listen to the dead voices."

They looked at each other.

"But what voices?" Brian broke in, sounding bewildered. "You've never dreamed about ghosts before, have you?"

Ollie and Coco shook their heads.

"And earlier," Brian continued, "Coco said she saw a ghost in the road coming up. But that was someone in a ski jacket. Three *different* ghosts?"

"I guess," said Coco, but now she looked doubtful.

"Maybe it's a coincidence?" said Brian. "Dreaming about a girl and her bones? You guys do hang out a lot. Maybe you would have the same dream."

"But then Mr. Voland shows up and tells us that the stories say this place is haunted by a woman and a little girl?" said Coco. "Like the ones in our dreams? That's a big coincidence."

Ollie didn't understand it, but she didn't think it was a coincidence.

"The ghosts behind the mist weren't dangerous," Brian continued. "Why would your watch say BEWARE now?"

"And then go blank," Coco chimed in. "It never did *that* before."

"I don't know," said Ollie. "I don't like it. I need a new way to talk to my mom. I thought—Mr. Voland seemed to know one. But now he's up there." Ollie glanced again back up into the dim stairwell.

Brian said, "Mr. Voland is a little weird, Owl. I wouldn't listen to everything . . ." He didn't finish his sentence. They had gotten to the bottom of the stairs.

Coco wrapped her arms around herself. "Did it get colder?"

Brian pulled his hoodie up over his head. Ollie did the same. "Colder? It's *freezing*."

It was. In the last ten minutes, the lobby had turned icy cold, as though the front door were standing open to the storm outside. But the door was shut tight.

"Guess the heat's out," said Ollie.

"But isn't it weird that it got this cold this fast?" Coco asked.

"Yup," said Brian.

They all exchanged glances.

Through the window in the front door, Ollie saw the torrent of falling snow. It looked like a wall. Keeping them there. The lobby fire was still out, but they went over to the hearth anyway.

"I'm going to talk to Mr. Voland when he comes back," said Ollie decisively. "I'm going to explain about my watch and ask him again how you talk to ghosts. We need to ask my mom what's going on, the sooner the better."

Coco nodded. But Brian was frowning. "Owl, why not

talk to your dad first? And Coco's mom. They're smart. Tell them about the watch and everything. Maybe they can help us figure this place out."

"My dad doesn't believe in ghosts," retorted Ollie. "He's not going to start believing just because we tell him. We have to figure out what's going on. And quickly! The last time my watch beeped, we were about to be grabbed and turned into scarecrows! We'll talk to my mom. She can help us."

Even though she was scared, Ollie felt a surge of hope and excitement at the thought.

Brian said, "Right. It's just—weird that you would trust Mr. Voland with the secret of the watch but not your dad."

"I'll tell my dad," said Ollie. "Eventually. We just don't know enough yet."

Brian looked unconvinced.

Just then, from the stairway came a soft whistle.

They all whipped around. The stairwell was empty.

Coco said, "Was that—is that Mrs. Wilson's bird clock?"

Ollie shook her head. "No."

"How do you know?" asked Brian.

"It only chimes on the hour," said Ollie. Her stomach felt hollow with fear.

"Then what—" whispered Coco. All three were staring up the stairs. Then they heard a laugh. A child's soft giggle. It seemed to come from everywhere. An icy wind whipped through the lobby. It felt suddenly to Ollie that every stuffed animal there was staring at them. She could see a lot of teeth.

Brian muttered, "The bear is on its hind legs now. Wasn't it—?"

"*What's happening?*" whispered Coco. The whistling came again, broke into a thin, tuneless sound. Stopped. There was a silence. The lobby was colder than ever. The giggle became a child's frightened wail, and the sound of small, hurrying feet.

Suddenly Coco gasped and pointed. The second-floor landing wasn't empty. A girl stood there. A girl in a long white nightgown. Her face was gray-white; her nose was black. Her eyes were frozen open, huge and unblinking.

They could see the darkness of the hallway behind her. Through her. She raised a hand. Her fingers were black with frostbite. Her lips moved. They didn't hear anything, but Ollie thought she recognized the words:

Don't listen.

Then more footsteps came racing up behind her. The girl shot a panicked look over her shoulder and disappeared.

Next second, they saw Mr. Voland, sprinting down the stairs, wild-eyed. He'd lost his glasses. He took the stairs two at a time, skidded to a halt in the center of the lobby, and bent over, elbows on his knees, shivering.

Ollie, Brian, and Coco went and crowded around him. "Mr. Voland," said Ollie. "Mr. Voland, what happened? Did you see her? The girl?"

Mr. Voland dragged in a deep breath and stood up. He was as pale as the snowstorm outside. He stared up the stairwell. Then, slowly, he lifted his hand, pulled down his sleeve. There were white marks on his arm. Like early frostbite.

"What girl? No. I found her," he said grimly. "Mother Hemlock. I think we're in trouble."

6

MR. VOLAND DIDN'T have time to say any more. Mrs. Wilson came bustling in, her arms full of firewood. "Goodness," she said brightly. "Look at you three just standing in the lobby. Tired of ghost hunting already?"

They all stared at her, and none of them said anything. Mrs. Wilson dropped her armful of sticks next to the cold fireplace. She knelt down in front of it. "Well, here goes nothing," she said. She pulled out a book of matches, struck one, and lit the tinder. A little curl of smoke came up. It flared and went dead.

"Allow me," said Mr. Voland. He knelt beside Mrs. Wilson. Coco noticed that his hands were shaking.

What had he seen upstairs? Coco wondered.

He did manage to light the tinder again, despite the shakes. He blew on it. Coco had seen Ollie's dad expertly start a lot of fires. She could see that Mr. Voland knew what he was doing. This time the tinder caught, and after a minute, the smaller sticks. Soon Mr. Voland had a small fire going. He stood up, dusting off his knees. He still looked afraid.

Coco sighed with relief herself. The fire felt like a little victory against the shadows, against the intense cold, against—whatever was upstairs. She felt grateful Mr. Voland was there, even if he was a little strange. She reached out and warmed her hands.

"Thank you, Don," said Mrs. Wilson stiffly. "Do you mind keeping the fire going for a bit? I have a lot to do."

"Don't mention it," said Mr. Voland. "Of course I will."

Mrs. Wilson hurried off.

"Why are we in trouble?" Ollie asked Mr. Voland. He was staring into the fireplace, watching the slow dance of the flames.

"Mr. Voland, what happened upstairs?" Coco asked.

Mr. Voland shrugged and answered them both, never taking his eyes off the fire. "Most ghosts—they just sort of exist. They're not people. More like the memory of a person. A piece of the past, stuck in the present. But sometimes—occasionally—they are more. Those ghosts don't just exist, they act. They want something. That's when they're dangerous, when they want something."

"Does Mother Hemlock want something?" Coco asked.

"Yes."

"What does she want?" Brian asked.

"I think," said Mr. Voland, with a glance at the staircase, "that she wants to keep us here."

"Why?" they all asked together.

"It will be dark in a few hours. Ghosts are stronger in the dark."

Coco shrank closer to her friends. The scarecrows in the world behind the mist had hunted in the dark.

"Okay then," said Ollie, saying what they were all thinking. "But what does she want to *do*? When she's stronger in the dark?"

"That is the question, isn't it?" Mr. Voland smiled down at them, but it wasn't a happy smile. "I fear the answer might be—unpleasant."

"But you said ghosts weren't dangerous," said Brian.

"The majority are not," said Mr. Voland crisply. "But the small remainder—can be. We should keep the fire going, if we can. They do not like firelight."

He wouldn't say anything else. He knelt and busied himself with the fire. After a minute, Ollie, Brian, and Coco went around to the dining room. The morning light had gone from the windows there. It was after noon, and the room looked cold and gray; shadows gathered in the corners, untouched by the tiny fire. The big dark mirror glimmered opposite the fireplace.

Brian said sharply, "What's that?" He was staring at the mirror. Coco and Ollie looked, but Coco didn't see anything. Just the dining room and their three tense faces.

"I don't see anything," said Ollie. "Brian, what was it?"

Brian shook his head, still staring at the mirror. He looked shaken. "I thought I saw her. In the mirror. The girl in the nightgown. She's gone now."

Coco looked through the big dining room window. At that time of year, she knew, it would start to get dark in only a few hours. The snow poured down outside.

Despite Mr. Voland's care, the fire was small and sullen. It sputtered. "What's wrong with the fire?" Coco asked. Ollie had a woodstove at home and knew a lot about fires.

"It's acting like the wood is wet," said Ollie. She went over to check the woodpile. "It's not, though." Another weird thing. Too many weird things, Coco thought. More than anything, she wanted to go home. But they couldn't, even if they wanted to. They were stuck.

Trapped, she thought, with an anxious glance at the staircase. *We're trapped*.

When the front door clattered open, they all jumped. Coco's mom and Ollie's dad came in, brushing snow from their hats and coats. Mr. Adler's beard was all frosted up, and they both had snow in their eyelashes.

"Lordy!" said Mr. Adler. "It's definitely snowing!" He stamped more snow off his boots, looked around. "And it's not much warmer in here than outside," he added. "Sue, is the heat not working either? How's the fire doing?"

Mrs. Wilson trudged back into the dining room. "Don just got the fire going again," she said, with a slightly friendlier nod at Mr. Voland. "Sam's trying to fix the heat. But . . ."

"Uh-huh. We couldn't fix the generators either," said Mr. Adler. "It was the strangest thing."

"What do you mean, strange?" Coco asked.

"There wasn't anything *wrong* with the generators," put in Coco's mom. She peeled off her ski jacket and shook the snow from her hair and coat. "At least, nothing that I could find. Except for not working, of course." She kicked snow off her own boots and went to the fire to warm her hands beside Coco. "How's it going, hon?" she asked.

"Okay," said Coco in a small voice. She debated telling her mother about what had happened in the upstairs hall. She decided not to. Her mom would just get annoyed at Mr. Voland for scaring them. She wouldn't actually believe they'd seen a ghost.

Mrs. Wilson said, "Well, I'll admit the heating has got

the same problem. It seems fine, everything looks good, the propane tanks are full. It's just not *heating*. We need to get an expert out, but . . ."

"But no one is getting through today," Ollie's dad finished. "Not until the storm ends." They all turned and looked out the dining room window. The storm didn't look like it planned to end anytime soon. Even with a small fire going, the lobby and dining room were still freezing. Coco wished she could go back upstairs for her ski jacket. But now she was scared of the long dark hallway, the rattling closet door, the black-dressed figure at the end of the hall, of Mr. Voland's voice: *she wants to keep us here.*

All the adults, Coco noticed, looked worried too.

She pulled out her phone. Twenty percent battery. She wished she'd grabbed her charging cable from the room. Too distracted by rattling closets. Coco sat down on the hearth beside the fireplace. *Mount Hemlock,* she typed into the search bar, *ghost.*

Maybe the internet knew something. Didn't it always?

She had to wait a long time for the page to load. The signal wasn't great, and there was no Wi-Fi with the power out. Coco thought longingly of doing homework at the Egg, with cinnamon rolls and fast internet.

Surprisingly, the first hit Coco saw wasn't even about the orphanage at all. Instead it was an article about a boy who'd gone missing five years ago.

MISSING on Mount Hemlock: Gabriel Bouvier, the article's headline read.

Coco clicked and read:

> **Mount Hemlock has long been closed to would-be skiers, standing as it does on the grounds of Sacred Heart Orphanage. But since the orphanage has been boarded up for decades, that has not stopped local youths from hiking in, hoping to climb the famously empty mountain and ski down.**
>
> **Now that adventurous pursuit may have claimed a victim.**

Coco kept reading. She saw a picture of an older boy in a blue ski jacket—the article said he was seventeen—with freckles and red hair, and a big smile.

> **Gabriel Bouvier disappeared while skiing alone in the vicinity of Mount Hemlock and Sacred Heart Orphanage. An extensive search is under way.**

Curious, Coco went to a later article. And another. *They never found him,* she realized.

"What are you reading, Coco?" Ollie asked.

Coco looked up and handed Ollie her phone. "Funny," she said. "I googled Mount Hemlock to see if I could find anything about ghosts. But if you google *Mount Hemlock ghost*, the first story is about someone named Gabriel Bouvier."

"Who?" said Brian, peering at her phone over Ollie's shoulder.

"He disappeared on the mountain a few years ago," said Coco. "Nothing to do with the orphanage at all. They never found him."

Brian and Ollie read the article together. When he'd finished, Brian looked up. "Coco," he said, "didn't you say the—person—maybe ghost—you saw on the road was . . ."

Coco had been waiting for someone to say it. "Was wearing a blue ski jacket," she finished. "With a ski mask, but no gloves."

"Gabriel Bouvier was wearing a blue ski jacket," Ollie said, scanning another article. "On the night he disappeared."

"Another ghost?" Coco asked, saying aloud what they were all thinking.

"Too many," said Brian darkly.

Ollie tried to click to another article. Frowned. "Hey, Coco, your phone says *no service* now. Not a single bar." Coco took her phone back. Ollie and Brian pulled out theirs. *No service,* said all three of their phones.

A chill of memory ran down Coco's spine. When the three found themselves in the world behind the mist, their phones had also stopped working. *No,* she reminded herself. *This isn't the same. We were alone last time. Now we have our parents, and the Wilsons and Mr. Voland.*

There was a crash from the front desk in the lobby. The trio looked over. Mrs. Wilson had slammed a phone receiver down. "Landlines are out," she said. "Storm must be knocking over phone lines too. If it goes on much longer, I guess we'll be buried here."

She said it like she was trying to make a joke. No one laughed.

Ollie's dad squinted down at his own phone. "I had service earlier today," he said. "Not anymore."

"Do you have a radio?" Coco's mom asked Mrs. Wilson. "A satellite phone?"

Mrs. Wilson, coming back into the dining room, shook her head. "They were going to be delivered on Thursday," she said. "I never dreamed . . ." She looked kind of helpless. Coco figured that she'd been ready to handle hordes of guests, but she didn't know what to do when they were snowed in without lights, heat, or a way to contact anyone.

"Okay," said Mr. Adler firmly. "This is fine. You hear me, kids? We are completely fine. Not a good time for nerves. You guys aren't nervous, are you?"

They were, but not in the way Mr. Adler was thinking.

"No, Dad," said Ollie clearly. "We're not nervous."

She gave Brian and Coco fierce looks, as though she were daring them to contradict her. *Don't go worrying my dad any more than he already is.* They didn't say anything. Although Brian looked like he really *wanted* to say something.

"Sue, you said there's plenty of firewood?" Ollie's dad asked.

She nodded.

"Great," said Mr. Adler. "And there's lots of food, I imagine, since you were planning on a lot of guests. Let's take a moment while we still have daylight and stack more firewood here near the hearth. We'll pile up blankets and spare batteries, sleep down here, and keep cozy near the fire until . . ."

Mr. Adler kept talking, making plans. But Ollie, Brian, and Coco had stopped listening. Ollie marched over to Mr. Voland. Brian and Coco followed her. He was standing apart from the other adults, and not helping them with the planning. He was watching the lobby stairwell.

"Mr. Voland," said Ollie, planting herself in front of him. "Do you think a ghost is doing it? Making the heat and power not work?"

"I imagine so," said Mr. Voland, not looking away from the stairs.

"Mother Hemlock?"

"Maybe."

"Why?" asked Coco.

"I don't know," said Mr. Voland. "Perhaps only to frighten us. Weaken us. Ghosts like it when you're afraid. It means you acknowledge them."

Somewhere out of sight, the bird clock whistled the hour.

And Ollie's watch began beeping again, frantically.

7

THE FOUR OF THEM jumped. The other adults were too far away to hear. Mr. Voland stared at Ollie's watch. "You need to tell me about that device on your wrist," he said.

Ollie put a protective hand on the watch face, muffling the noise. Brian and Coco stood silent on either side of her. "Why?" she demanded.

Mr. Voland looked stern. "I believe we are in danger," he said. "We cannot leave. We don't have light, we don't have heat, and the ghost upstairs is strong, and will only get stronger as the sun sets. I do not know what she wants. Are you willing to bet that she's harmless?"

The three didn't say anything.

Mr. Voland went on in a softer voice. "We need every advantage," he said. "That"—one long finger pointed at Ollie's watch—"is no ordinary device; I'd stake my life on it." The watch was beeping so fast now that it was almost like a continuous buzz. Ollie glanced down and saw letters rippling over its pale gray surface faster than ever. But they didn't stop long enough for her to make sense of them.

Still Ollie hesitated. Except for Brian and Coco, she'd never told anyone about her watch. Not even her dad. It was too strange, and too precious, and too painful. But she met Mr. Voland's strange two-colored eyes, and abruptly she found the story spilling out.

"My watch helps me," she said. "When I—when we were in danger the last time, my watch told me what to do. My watch was—it was my mother's. I think she talks to me with it. I think she's trying to warn us now."

Brian and Coco were silent, although Brian was frowning.

"Ah," said Mr. Voland with a sigh. "That explains it. You have a very powerful object there, Ollie. I trust you keep it safe?"

"Yes," said Ollie. She was on the edge of tears, and she almost never cried. "But I don't know what to *do* now. I don't know what it's trying to say."

"Don't worry," said Mr. Voland. "We'll contact your mother and ask. Perhaps she will tell us what is happening and what we must do."

Brian just scowled at Mr. Voland. "How are we going to do that?" he demanded, just as Ollie asked, "Now?"

"Tonight," Mr. Voland. "I have a method. We'll have to do it after dark, unfortunately. It's not something you can do when the sun is up. But as soon as we can, after the sun sets. And I will show you how."

Brian opened his mouth, closed it again. Ollie nodded once. "Let's do it. Just—don't tell my dad." Ollie didn't know what her dad would do if she told him she was going to try and talk to her mom. Would he be happy or sad or angry, tell her not to, or want to help? It was better, Ollie decided, not to worry him. Not until she *knew*.

"Very well," said Mr. Voland, "but I think there are plans afoot for everyone to spend the night in the lobby. Because of the chill. We will have to be very quiet if you wish to hide this from your father, Ollie."

"I don't like it," Brian said abruptly. "Why should we lie to Ollie's dad?"

"Do you want to explain it to him?" asked Mr. Voland coolly.

"We could try," said Brian, stubborn. "Maybe he'd listen."

"Or maybe—" began Mr. Voland, but just then, Ollie's dad interrupted them.

He and Ms. Zintner were putting armloads of firewood

by the fireplace. He called across the room, "Ollie-pop, can you three go upstairs and nab all your warm clothes and the blankets off your beds? We're going to have to sleep near the fireplace tonight. It's the only proper heat source, with the heaters not working."

They all went tense. No one wanted to go back up the stairs. But Ollie's dad had already bounced outside to pick up another armload of firewood without waiting for an answer.

"What do we do?" Ollie asked.

"There is a good deal we don't know," said Mr. Voland. "But certainly we must neither be foolhardy nor give in to panic. We do need coats and blankets. Clean socks and phone chargers. Better we go upstairs now than after nightfall."

The three of them nodded reluctant agreement. Ollie stared across the lobby, toward the staircase. It disappeared upward into thick blackness. *Why is it so dark up there?* Ollie wondered. *Much too dark. It can't be that close to sunset yet.*

"Let's go now," Mr. Voland said. "The sooner the better. Don't worry, I'll come with you." He gave the kids a sudden, warm smile. Ollie found herself feeling better. "I advise you to hold hands," said Mr. Voland as they headed for the stairs. "And," he added under his breath, almost too low for the kids to hear, "whatever you see, don't let go."

———

The rattling closet was quiet as they passed it. There were no strange shadows on the floor, and no dark figure at the end of the corridor. The four of them held hands, and they walked quickly.

And walked.

And walked.

The corridor never seemed to get any shorter.

It was Brian who whispered first, tugging on their hands, "Guys. Guys, shouldn't we have gotten to the rooms by now?"

They all halted. "It's true, we have been walking a long time," said Mr. Voland doubtfully. "But—"

He looked around him. The light was a deep charcoal-gray. It was not perfectly dark, but not far from it either. The only illumination came from the fading, snow-filled daylight in the big windows at either end of the long hall.

Suddenly Coco asked, "Are anyone's feet wet?"

"How could they be?" asked Brian reasonably. "None of us has been outside."

"Then," Coco said in a small voice, *"who made the footprints?"*

Ollie looked down the hall and saw what Coco had—that a line of wet footprints followed them.

"Are you three *sure* no one has tracked in snow?" asked Mr. Voland.

"No!" Brian snapped. His voice cracked with anxiety and impatience. "If we said we didn't, we didn't. None of us has been outside."

Ollie's eye kept tracking the line of wet footprints.

They stopped right next to her.

Ollie looked up. A big mirror hung across from them. In the dark hall, their reflections were only shadowy outlines.

There were five outlines.

But there were only four of them in the hallway.

It took Ollie a moment to understand. She spun in a circle, searching. "Guys!" she cried. "Look, the mirror! Someone's here! Someone's in the hall with us!"

Coco was still clinging to Ollie's left hand; Ollie had Brian's cold fingers in her right. She couldn't see anyone around them. Not in the hallway. Just her and Brian and Coco and Mr. Voland. But in the mirror, a fifth shape stood among them.

"What is it?" cried Coco.

"It's only in the mirror," said Brian.

Brian was on Coco's left, Ollie realized. He wasn't next to her at all.

"Whose hand am I holding?" Ollie whispered. She

looked to her right and saw nothing. "Whose hand am I holding?" she cried. She couldn't see anything. But icy fingers still gripped hers tight. Ollie looked straight in the mirror to see, dimly, a torn blue ski jacket, a face hidden by a ski mask.

All four of them saw it. They stared, frozen.

Mr. Voland said to the fifth reflection, in a shaken voice, "Whatever you are, can you talk to us?"

No answer. Just a silhouette, black in the darkened mirror.

"Can it hurt us?" Coco whispered.

"I don't know," Mr. Voland replied. He took a step closer, peering through his glasses.

"Run!" cried Ollie. "Guys, run—I can't move—it's *holding my hand!*" She tugged, but the thing wouldn't let go. A creeping horror started to overtake her: a feeling that, if she stayed there long enough, she would become a reflection instead of a girl. She felt herself take an involuntary step toward that dark mirror, then another.

But she didn't take a third. Instead Mr. Voland pushed her aside, wrapped his jacket around his hand, and smashed the mirror.

The cold grip on Ollie's hand relaxed and vanished, leaving white spots on her skin, almost like frostbite. The mirror was broken, and they were alone in the hallway. Ollie couldn't stop shivering.

"Look," said Coco in a strained whisper. "We were at the end of the corridor, after all. Our door—our door is right here. It was right here the whole time."

Ollie remembered suddenly the rest of a warning she'd heard in a nightmare.

Stay out of closets. And don't look in the mirror.

She looked down, but her watch face was still blank. Her hand hurt, and she couldn't stop shaking.

8

THEY GRABBED BLANKETS, coats, knit caps, and warm socks, and hurried back to the lobby. They didn't look into any mirrors; they didn't stop at any closets. Mr. Voland went last, casting cautious glances over his shoulder the whole time. Ollie was grateful for Mr. Voland. A line of cuts ran across his knuckles from the broken glass.

In the lobby, the first thing Ollie saw was the silly canoe with its three paddling raccoons; their unexpected, sharp-toothed smiles gave her a jolt. The canoe was sitting next to the front desk, facing the stairwell, as though the raccoons were guarding the bright bowls of candy and matchbooks on the front desk. Hadn't the raccoons been over the fireplace before? Maybe Mrs. Wilson had moved them.

Whatever. Ollie, tired of weirdness, marched over to them, grabbed a matchbook and a handful of candy, and shoved them both in her pocket. Never knew when matches would come in handy. And even if she was still cold and shivering from what had happened upstairs, she wasn't going to be afraid of stupid stuffed *raccoons*.

The raccoons looked like they were laughing. Ollie swerved away from them, headed toward the double entrance doors, shoved them open, and went outside. She stood in her sneakers under the dry, freezing portico, glad to breathe the outside air, even if it was full of snow. The wind had dropped. But the snow hadn't let up. Not even a little. It fell down in sheets as fast as rain. It lay in drifts almost as high as the dining room window. Ollie couldn't even tell which lumps in the parking lot were Susie or Mr. Voland's car. She scrubbed her right hand, the hand the ghost had touched, hard in the snow.

Coco poked her head out. "Come on, Ollie," she said. "You okay? Come inside. It's freezing." Coco had already put her ski jacket on over her sweatshirt, and she still looked cold.

But Ollie didn't move; she was staring out over the parking lot with longing. *Maybe*, she thought, *we can dig out Susie and sleep in her, with the heat going*. But even as she thought it, Ollie knew they couldn't. They needed the gas to get home. They were stuck inside the lodge. Reluctantly, she followed Coco back inside.

Ollie's dad was wearing his ski jacket and knit hat

indoors. The tip of his nose was bright red with the chill. "Shut the door!" he called to Ollie as she came in.

Ollie pulled the door shut. Her dad was kneeling in front of the fireplace on the lobby side, and he had gotten the fire going a little better. It glowed yellow instead of red and threw out a small circle of heat. There was the friendly sound of logs snapping. Someone had also collected a lot of battery-powered lamps and set them up around the hearth. The lamps pushed back the shadows, made a ring of warm light. Ollie went toward the fireplace. Brian, Coco, and Mr. Voland were already there, putting down their loads of coats and blankets.

"Thanks for grabbing these," Ollie's dad said to them, clambering to his feet. He helped them make a neat stack of blankets and pillows near the fire. "You guys want to be in charge of bed setup later on? Great, excellent."

He didn't wait for answers, but headed at once over to the kitchen. They could hear him talking to Mr. Wilson. Since the gas wasn't working, they had to decide what cold stuff would be best for dinner. "How's your stash of peanut butter?" her dad was asking brightly.

"Thanks for breaking the mirror," said Ollie awkwardly to Mr. Voland. "It—whatever it was—didn't let me go until you did."

Mr. Voland was shaking out a blanket.

"Don't mention it," he said. "You were very brave."

"We've seen worse," said Ollie. They had. The mirror had been bad, but the scarecrows behind the mist had been worse.

Mr. Voland's eyes narrowed. But he didn't ask. Ollie was glad he didn't. He put the blanket down next to the fireplace and flexed his cut hand. "Although," Mr. Voland added with a faint smile, "I do not know how I am going to explain the broken mirror to Sue."

"Say it was a ghost," said Ollie.

"I guess I'll have to," he replied, and they both laughed a little. "The three of you should stay downstairs and stay together for the rest of the day," Mr. Voland added to the whole trio. "Promise?"

All three promised. But then Brian, scowling, headed over to the front desk and grabbed the whole bowl of candy. "Okay, but I need some candy," he said.

"Are we allowed?" asked Coco.

"Today we are," said Brian, plunking the bowl down on the hearth by the fire and starting to make himself a blanket nest to sit in. "No skiing *and* ghosts? There is no limit to the peanut butter cups that I am allowed to consume."

"Seconded," said Ollie, and reached for one. "I just had a ghost grab my hand."

Coco shrugged agreement and ate a Snickers. She'd brought her travel chess set downstairs with the blankets. "Ollie, want to play?"

Ollie didn't really feel like chess, but it was better than peering into the shadows or sitting and watching the light fade out of the dining room windows.

Ollie and Coco played for a while, trading matches back and forth, neither of them trying very hard. Brian watched them play and read *The Voyage of the Dawn Treader.* Ollie kept stealing glances at the dragon-headed ship on the book's cover. She wanted to be on a ship right then, with no walls, only water, and a hot sun overhead.

Mr. Voland had settled down at one of the dining room tables—with a view through the archway to the stairs. Sometimes he wrote in a little notebook, but mostly he stared through the archway. Once Ollie lifted her head from the chess game, after she'd just checkmated a distracted Coco, to see him watching the three of them.

"Do you play chess?" Ollie asked Mr. Voland.

"You can play, if you want," Coco chimed in. She was always hunting for new opponents.

"Yes," said Mr. Voland. "I play." He smiled at them both. "I like games. But I fear I'd be too much for you. Enjoy your fun."

Coco looked like she wanted to challenge Mr. Voland

to a chess duel then and there. But before she could say anything, Ollie's dad made an entrance from the kitchen with a huge plate piled high with graham crackers, chocolate, and marshmallows.

"S'mores!" cried Coco, distracted.

"Hm," said Ollie's dad, "you three can't possibly be hungry after all that candy." He cast an eye on the floor, which was scattered with wrappers.

"Dad—" said Ollie.

"But I'll leave this here anyway," her dad went on, depositing the platter by the fire. "Keep it safe for me?"

"No worries there," said Brian, and they all gathered around the fire. Making s'mores was always fun. Carefully, they skewered their marshmallows. Ollie and Coco laughed at Brian, who could never manage to toast a marshmallow without catching it on fire. "It's fine," Brian insisted. "Catching it on fire cooks it just as well." To illustrate, he sandwiched his blackened marshmallow between slabs of graham cracker and chocolate and took a giant bite. Ollie and Coco, still laughing, hurried to toast theirs too.

They ate until they couldn't eat any more. S'mores took their minds off things. But eventually they put the last of the graham crackers and chocolate aside. When the fun stopped, the twilight seemed to rush in.

The light outside was blue-violet, and somewhere

beyond the mountains the sun sank. The day shuddered to a gray and strange close.

Ollie's dad and Ms. Zintner had been in and out all afternoon, messing with the generator, checking on the fire. If they'd seen anything strange, they hadn't said. And it didn't seem like they had. Mr. Adler was just as cheerful as usual. It was only Ollie, Brian, Coco, and Mr. Voland who seemed to have noticed anything wrong.

Even though Mr. Voland had carefully nursed the fire along, the lodge kept getting colder.

"Why is it so cold?" Ollie asked Mr. Voland. All that afternoon, when he wasn't feeding the fire, he'd barely taken his eyes off the lobby stairwell. She was pretty sure the other grown-ups were annoyed with him. He hadn't offered to help bring in firewood, and he wasn't hunting for ghosts, like he said he meant to. But Ollie thought he was doing something. He was keeping watch.

"A cold spot is a sure sign of supernatural activity," Mr. Voland replied. "I suspect that a thermometer would show the room reading at a much warmer temperature than it feels."

"What can we do?" Ollie asked.

"Stay together," said Mr. Voland. "Keep the fire burning. And hope the night holds answers as well as danger." He put another log on the sullen flames.

Ollie hoped so too. She touched her watch. It had been silent for hours now. But she hoped it wasn't done telling her things. She hoped she'd talk to her mom that night. She felt a little thrill of excitement at the thought.

"Ollie!" called her dad from the kitchen.

Ollie, a little reluctantly, left Mr. Voland and the fireplace. With its small windows, the kitchen was even darker than the dining room. Her dad was working by the light of a battery-powered lamp, slathering peanut butter and jelly on bread. "Grab the mayonnaise jar," he told her, "and throw us together some ham sandwiches. I'm sorry we're stuck eating cold sandwiches two nights running, but the propane's not working—we can't use the stove. At least there's plenty of dry goods." He tweaked one of Ollie's curls. "Can't live on s'mores."

Actually, Ollie wasn't too hungry—she'd eaten a *lot* of s'mores. But she picked up a spreader and a piece of bread anyway. Making food with her dad was familiar; it made her feel better. Her dad loved to feed people. Mr. Wilson had left him in charge of the cooking. Which made sense, Ollie thought with pride. Her dad was a much better cook.

Ollie spread mayonnaise on bread, laid down neat slices of ham. As she did, she looked around the kitchen. It had big, new metal counters, metal sinks. A giant gas range with eight burners. She wished they could light the stove and have soup. But that wasn't working either.

In the corner, Ollie caught sight of a skinny door. The knob was dented. It was hard to see it in the shadows.

"Where does that door go?" Ollie asked, pointing.

"Sam says it goes to the basement," said her dad. "But it's full of rusty nails and old axes and other sharp things—maybe hold off on exploring until tomorrow?"

"Don't have to tell me twice," said Ollie with feeling. No way was she going into a moldy old basement.

They finished their sandwiches and took them out to the others, along with chips and apples and oranges. Ms. Zintner was trying to boil water in a pot awkwardly hung over the fire, but it didn't work. Ollie caught herself thinking, *My mom would have known what to do,* but she tried to quash the thought. It wasn't Ms. Zintner's fault that they couldn't boil water. The fire didn't get that hot. It stayed low and sullen and smoky, and the smoke, instead of going straight up, crept sideways into their eyes.

———

"Dad, do you think the storm will stop tomorrow?" Ollie asked after they'd finished eating their sandwiches. It was inky, snow-filled night by then. A couple of the battery-powered lamps had already died, and none of the fresh batteries could get them to light again. All eight people in the lodge had drawn in close around the fire, staying in its hoop of light and warmth. Ollie was sitting on a blanket next to her dad's chair, leaning her head on his knee like a little kid. Even her dad looked tired now. He had been joking and singing all that long afternoon as the lodge got colder and colder. He'd kept them all laughing. But now there were purple pouches under his eyes.

"I don't know, Ollie-pop," he said simply. "I've never seen a storm like this. But it'll be okay. The storm has to stop eventually. We have walls and a roof and blankets and plenty of food and firewood. We'll be all right."

Ollie said, "Dad—have you *ever* believed in ghosts?"

Her dad frowned down at her, pulling at a splinter that had lodged itself in his thumb. Ollie wished she hadn't asked. He'd been worried that day too. Worried about different things. About keeping her and Brian and Coco fed and warm and not scared.

Her dad said seriously, "I believe in memory. I believe in remembering someone you love so well that it becomes kind of like a ghost. You remember someone so hard that it feels like they're in the next room, just around the corner, that they could walk in any minute. But the kind of ghosts that Mr. Voland says he's looking for? The ghosts that walk up and down, like Jacob Marley in *A Christmas*

Carol? No. I don't believe in ghosts like that. You have to decide what you believe, Ollie-pop. That's part of growing up. But . . ." He bent down and whispered in her ear. "I wouldn't listen too much to Mr. Voland. Dead people, they're gone. They've left us, except for the part of them that we carry around forever."

Ollie only nodded once. "Okay," she said very softly. They both stared into the glowing coals of the feeble fire. "I love you."

Gently, her dad stroked her hair as they watched the fire sputter and sink low in the darkness.

———

More of the battery-powered lamps had gone out. They were down to two. The small fire made the shadows dance along the walls of the dining room. Coco tried not to watch the shadows. She kept expecting to see a human figure there, a long arm pointing.

Coco *really* didn't want it to get dark.

"Hey, Coco," said her mom. "Can you help me straighten up these blankets?"

Coco went over. Her mom was rearranging the piles of pillows and comforters so that everyone would have a spot to sleep, as near to the fire as they could get. Ollie, Coco, and Brian, plus Coco's mom and Mr. Adler, would be on the dining room side of the fire. Mr. Voland and the Wilsons would be on the lobby side.

"How are you doing, sweetie?" her mom asked as Coco shook out blankets. "Here, let's put you three kids a bit closer to the fire." Her mom smiled crookedly. "Some vacation, huh?"

"Mom, I'm scared," Coco said. She didn't want to admit it to Ollie or Brian. She wanted to be brave for them, because they were being brave for her. They were joking with Ollie's dad and keeping an eye on the staircase without saying anything about being afraid. But she could admit it to her mother.

"There's nothing to be scared of," said her mom, smoothing the corner of a blanket. "It might not be the most fun because it's so chilly in here and we're kind of stuck. But there's nothing to be scared of."

"We saw a ghost in the hallway upstairs," Coco said in a small voice.

Her mother pressed her lips together. "The imagination is a very powerful thing, sweetheart," she said. She shot Mr. Voland an annoyed look. "It might have been a mistake to let you go ghost hunting."

"But—why is it so cold, and why is everything breaking?" Coco demanded. "We *did* see a ghost. I—I think all this is the ghost's fault."

"Things are breaking because of the snowstorm," said her mom more gently, putting aside the last blanket. "And you are safe. Roger and I—we won't let anything happen to you."

Coco felt better. But only a little.

"Like Roger said," Coco's mom went on, "we have plenty of supplies. We'll be okay until the storm stops."

Coco wanted to believe it. They were all together. Five grown-ups. It wasn't like the last time, when she and Ollie and Brian had been all alone, and lost and running.

But she was still afraid.

———

The second-to-last battery-powered lamp went out, and Ollie's dad said, still with his determined cheerfulness, "Well, I think that's probably our signal to go to bed."

Despite the fire, it was so cold in the dining hall that they all breathed out plumes like dragons in the frosty air.

Mr. Voland said, "I think I will sit up awhile longer."

"Suit yourself," said Ollie's dad.

They went to the downstairs bathroom to brush their teeth. On their way back, Ollie murmured to Mr. Voland, "What happens now?"

"Try and get some rest," he said. "Don't sleep—stay alert. I'll get you when it's time."

Ollie nodded. The shadows pressed in while they settled under their covers. The fire threw flickering shadows across the walls and ceiling of the dining room.

Ollie, Brian, and Coco settled in side by side, wrapped tightly in blankets. When they were settled, Brian said, whispering, "Ollie, I still don't think this talking-to-ghosts thing is a good idea."

"Do you have a better idea?" Ollie asked. "We can trust Mr. Voland. He broke the mirror for me, and he's been keeping watch all day. I think we'd be in real trouble if it weren't for him!"

"Maybe so," conceded Brian. "But still. It doesn't feel right. Dead people—they're gone. We aren't meant to talk to them."

Brian, Coco remembered, was Catholic. It came out at odd moments.

Ollie rolled over onto her back and stared at the ceiling, jaw set. "Stay in bed if you don't want to help," she said.

"I never said—" Brian began.

"Cut it *out*," whispered Coco. "We're about to have a pretty darn rough night, it seems like. It won't help if you two are arguing over this. We have to watch each other's backs. And, Brian, I don't really like this either, but I can't think of a better way. Ollie, Brian is trying to help us. Even if he doesn't agree with you, that's no reason to be mean."

There was a small silence. Then, "Sorry," Brian whispered.

"I'm sorry too," said Ollie.

No one said anything else. Somewhere out of sight, the bird clock whistled the hour. Side by side, they lay on their backs and watched the firelight fade from gold to red as the fire burned low.

9

OLLIE LAY STIFF and open-eyed on her hard bed of blankets. There was the smell of new carpet under her head. Her dad had turned the last battery-powered lamp off to save it from just dying on them. Ollie had worn her hoodie to bed, along with her beanie, a long-sleeved shirt, flannel pants, and long, thick socks. Even under the blankets, all that was barely enough to keep her warm.

The fire burned a sullen dark red. Ollie lay still, watching the slow waltz of the red light across the ceiling of the dining room.

She couldn't sleep. She felt like every single one of her nerves was strung as tight as the lines of the storm-wrapped ski lifts outside. She was waiting. Listening. Beside her she could feel her friends, as tense and as open-eyed as she was. For a while they heard the murmur of the adults' voices; once, Ollie's dad laughed softly.

But slowly the adults went off to bed; their voices dropped away. Then it was only silence that filled the lobby and the dining room of Hemlock Lodge. Silence except for the sound of the storm. It was so strange, Ollie thought vaguely, how the storm could sound just like a person. Now, for example, the wind sounded like a soft, steady whimpering, going on and on and on, like a human voice circling Hemlock Lodge, looking for a way in.

And then Ollie must have fallen asleep, even though she'd told Mr. Voland she wouldn't. Because now she realized that the whimpering wasn't the wind at all. It was a girl in a long white nightgown, crouching in a corner of the dining room, her arms wrapped about her skinny knees, crying.

In her dream, Ollie got up and went to the girl. All around them, Hemlock Lodge wasn't a newly renovated ski lodge anymore. It was a ruin. Ollie saw holes in the wall; her feet crunched on broken glass. The splintery floor snagged on her socks. In her dream, she shook with cold.

"Why are you crying?" Ollie asked the girl in the corner.

The girl lifted her face. Ollie couldn't suppress a shudder at the bloodless skin, the nose black with frostbite.

"I want to go home," said the girl.

Ollie knelt down beside her. "Where is your home?" she asked.

The girl gnawed on her lower lip. "I don't know," she whispered. "I can't remember. But it's somewhere. It has to be somewhere, doesn't it?"

"It's somewhere," said Ollie soothingly. "I'll help you find it."

The girl made a strange, broken sound, halfway between a laugh and a whimpering sob. "How?" she demanded. "Home's not here. There's nothing but dark here. I can't get out!" The girl's voice rose suddenly to a scream. "I can't get out! I can't leave until I find my bones. But they're nowhere."

Ollie was desperate to stop the girl's sobbing. "No," she said, stammering. "No, don't cry. I'll help you get out. I'll help. I'll help you find your bones."

The girl stared at Ollie with huge eyes as black as dead coals, and she laughed, a low, terrible sound. "Help me?" she whispered, with freezing scorn. "*You* help me? How? You're trapped just as much as me."

"No," Ollie started to say. "No I'm not—"

But the girl had leaped to her feet. "Trapped!" she screamed. Her mouth fell open; her teeth and tongue were blackened. "Trapped, trapped, trapped! You dummy! You'll stay here forever, until you're old bones just like me!"

She whirled and sprinted across the dining room, her nightgown a spot of white in the gloom. Ollie clambered to her feet and tried to follow. But she found her way blocked. A woman, dressed all in black, stood in front of her.

"Where do you think you're going, missy?" A bony hand closed on Ollie's arm.

Ollie tried to scream and lurched awake, gasping. For a few racing breaths, she did not know where she was. Then she remembered. She was lying in a bed made of blankets. *Dining room. Hemlock Lodge. Mountain. Storm. Ghosts.*

Mom.

With that, Ollie's head cleared. She was so tired of nightmares. She sat up slowly.

Mr. Voland was still sitting at his table a good distance from the hearth, just at the edge of the farthest reach of the firelight. The low scarlet coals of the fire threw strange shadows over his face, and reddened his skin. Everything was completely still. Ollie wondered how long she'd slept. She could hear her dad snoring faintly. Ms. Zintner slept curled up, an arm over her head.

Mr. Voland saw Ollie awake, put a finger to his lips, and beckoned, wordless.

Ollie nodded and turned to shake Brian and Coco. They sat up, not talking, rubbing their faces sleepily. They were going to have to be as quiet as they possibly could, to not wake anyone up, Ollie thought. *Be quiet,* she mouthed at her friends, then got up and went to Mr. Voland.

"Has anything happened?" she breathed.

Mr. Voland didn't say anything in reply. Instead he cupped a hand over his ear and put a finger over his lips at the same time. *Hush and listen,* he was saying. Brian and Coco had followed Ollie across to where Mr. Voland waited.

Now they listened.

The lodge was still, except—what was that? It sounded like the wind. The storm wind crying around Hemlock Lodge, just like it had been doing all day.

But in Ollie's dream, the noise hadn't been the wind. It had been a ghost girl with frostbite on her face, crying in a corner. It sounded like someone was crying now. Like someone upstairs and out of sight was crying. She looked at Brian and Coco, saw them thinking the same thing.

The wind, Brian mouthed at Mr. Voland.

Don only shrugged. *Maybe.*

Ollie's palms were sweating.

Don gestured to something he'd set up on the table in front of him. Then he pointed to three chairs. Carefully, they sat down. Ollie glanced back at her dad. He was still snoring away, which surprised her a little. Her dad wasn't that heavy a sleeper. But they'd been quiet.

They needed to hurry. On cold nights, Ollie's dad was used to getting up every few hours, going downstairs, and adding logs to their woodstove to make sure the house stayed warm until morning. Her dad would wake up soon to check on the fire.

Somewhere above them, the sobbing sound went on and on. Ollie felt the hairs on her arms standing up.

The table in front of them held three things.

The first thing was an empty cardboard box. Brian picked it up and tilted it into the red firelight so that all three of them could read what was printed on it.

OUIJA, it said.

Below that, in smaller letters, it said, MYSTIFYING ORACLE.

Brian frowned. "A Ouija board?" he breathed, in the smallest, softest whisper he could manage. "Isn't that just—a party game?"

"It can be," murmured Mr. Voland, his voice as soft as Brian's. "But it also works for its intended purpose. Talking to ghosts."

The Ouija board itself was laid on the table beside its box. It had two parts. Ollie had to squint to see them. The first part was the big wooden board. Mr. Voland's Ouija board was shiny and smooth, as though it had been touched by many hands. A picture was carved into each of the board's four corners: a smiling sun, a frowning moon, a black bird, and a woman with her arms folded, who appeared to be asleep.

120

The middle of the board was carved with the alphabet. To the right and left, above the alphabet, were the words YES and NO. Below the alphabet were the numbers 1 through 9 and 0.

Below that was a single word, carved deep. GOODBYE.

This board was the first piece.

The second piece was small. It looked like a magnifying glass with an arrow on one side. It was lying in the middle of the board, right on G.

Mr. Voland pointed to it. "This is the planchette," he breathed. "It indicates the letters. Everyone put your two forefingers on it with me."

They did, except for Brian. Brian looked unconvinced. He had picked up the Ouija board's box, which had instructions printed on the inside of the lid. Brian turned the instructions toward the firelight and started reading them.

Mr. Voland looked just the faintest bit annoyed. "We do not have much time."

"I just want to know what we're getting into." Brian was whispering, but not as quietly as the others. Ollie glared at him. Did he *want* her dad or Coco's mom to wake up? The soft sobbing of the wind—or not the wind—seemed to have crept closer. But still Brian was reading over the instructions like he didn't have a care in the world. Ollie felt herself starting to get annoyed at Brian.

"We have to hurry," Ollie told him.

Brian was still running a finger down the instructions. His finger paused at the bottom. His frown deepened. "There are four warnings."

"*Warnings?*" asked Coco.

"Yes," said Brian. "'One: don't use the board alone.'"

"We aren't going to," murmured Mr. Voland. He sounded like he was struggling to keep his patience. Behind them, Ollie's dad snorted and turned over in his sleep. Ollie gave Brian an agonized glance. He went right on reading.

"'Two: don't use the board in a graveyard.'"

Ollie shook her head impatiently. *No graves here.* Coco said nothing.

"'Three,'" said Brian. "'Just because the board says something doesn't mean it's true.'"

"However," broke in Mr. Voland, "I can tell you when the board is—" The sound of someone stirring in their sleep near the fire silenced him.

"'Four,'" said Brian. "'Always say goodbye.'"

There was a pause.

"Why? What does that mean?" Ollie asked. Involuntarily, her eye went again to GOODBYE, stark at the bottom of the board.

"Because," Mr. Voland said shortly, "if you don't move the planchette to GOODBYE, they do not necessarily depart."

"The ghosts don't leave?" Coco whispered. Ollie

frowned. Outside, the wind moaned to itself. Brian was watching Mr. Voland, narrow-eyed.

"But," Mr. Voland said, "we will always say goodbye. Now if you have had quite enough chitchat? We'll begin."

After a long pause, Ollie shook herself and nodded.

Brian was looking at that big, black **GOODBYE** burned into the wood at the bottom of the Ouija board. He cocked his head, listening to the faint, strange sobbing that might not be the storm. They all waited for him.

Finally Brian nodded. He still looked unhappy. But he put his hands on the planchette too.

"Now," said Mr. Voland. He was talking so low that he was barely moving his lips. All of them had to bend forward, hardly breathing, in order to hear him. "You will close your eyes, breathe evenly, and concentrate. Ollie, you must take the lead here. When you feel ready, ask a question."

Ollie nodded, closed her eyes, and thought about her mom. *That* wasn't hard. Her mom had been the best. Fierce, reckless, brilliant. A math professor, an adventurer. Everything Ollie wanted to be when she grew up. Always laughing, always running, always flying. When Dad told Ollie her mom's plane had fallen out of the sky, it had taken Ollie forever to believe it. Her mother couldn't be gone. How could a pine box in a church contain all that life? Her mom wasn't there. She had to be somewhere else. Perhaps behind a tree, behind a doorway, perhaps just in the space where the shadows met the firelight.

Ollie opened her eyes suddenly. With two fingers on the planchette, she whispered, softer than a sigh, "Are you here?"

Mr. Voland's lighter eye gleamed with the red light of the low, sputtering fire. His darker eye seemed coal-black.

They waited. Nothing.

Ollie's voice cracked a little as she said it a second time: "*Mom. Are you here?*"

Suddenly, the little piece of wood began to move. It quivered. And then it started a slow slide from letter to letter.

"*N*," said Coco, reading aloud. "*E. A.*"

"Near, it means near," said Ollie. Her heart raced. The wind (or not the wind) moaned. Her dad sighed and turned over in his sleep. The planchette swung up to YES.

"In life, did you belong to this orphanage?" murmured Mr. Voland.

Another pause. Then the planchette went to NO. It quivered again.

A strange, buoyant, impossible hope was rising in Ollie's chest. "Who are you, then?" she asked.

The planchette moved almost at once that time. HELLO OLIVIA, it said. Only her mom had ever called her Olivia.

"Mom?" Ollie whispered. "Mom?" Her heart was beating faster and faster. "Mom, where are you?"

The planchette hesitated. Then it started to swing once more. BEWARE, it said.

Brian's hands twitched on the planchette.

"Mom—what's happening?" Ollie breathed. Her heart was going like a hummingbird's wings. "Why—beware? What's wrong with this place?"

"One question at a time, Ollie," said Mr. Voland.

GHOSTS WANT TO KEEP YOU HERE, spelled the planchette.

"How?" Ollie whispered. "Why?"

Brian was scowling mistrustfully at the Ouija board, but Ollie didn't care. Her entire concentration was locked on the planchette under her fingers. She wished it would spell faster. "What do I do?"

MIRROR, said the planchette. LOOK MIRROR. ANSWER IN MIRROR.

All four of them stared up at the mirror. It hung almost directly in front of them, opposite the fireplace, big and dark. Ollie could see the red coals of the fire reflected in it. And, dimly, the dark shapes of chairs and tables and their own faces. What else? Was there something else?

"Owl," said Brian, low.

Ollie ignored him. She got up and took a step closer to the mirror. Before she could take another, Brian's hand fell heavily on her shoulder. "Ollie, where are you going?" Brian wasn't even bothering to be quiet now. "Remember the mirror upstairs? *Be careful.*"

Ollie shot an agonized glance at her sleeping dad, but still, strangely, none of the adults stirred. She threw off Brian's hand and took another step toward the mirror. "I just want to see, Brian," she whispered. "That was my mom. She was talking to me. I'm careful."

"Owl," said Brian. "*Don't believe everything the board tells you.*"

"It's my mom. She called me Olivia. Only my mom ever called me that," Ollie retorted. "We believed my watch when we were in the corn maze. I'm going to believe the board now. What else do we have to believe in? How else are we going to figure this out? I'm just going to look. Come with me if you want to help."

Ollie's dad murmured something in his sleep. It sounded like *Ollie.*

"Hang on—" Brian began.

"*Guys,*" broke in Coco. To Ollie, it sounded like she'd been trying to get their attention for a while. "Guys, listen."

Ollie and Brian fell silent. And they heard it. A tap.

Tap.

Where was it coming from?

Then Ollie realized it was coming from the mirror.

Someone was tapping on the mirror. But who? Ollie took another step, craning to see.

Mr. Voland watched with slitted eyes.

Tap. Tap.

"Ollie," said Brian, still following her, "*please* be careful."

"It's okay. I'm careful," she whispered back. She stared into the glimmering depths of the mirror so hard that her eyes watered.

Behind her, she heard Mr. Voland talking. "Don't worry, Coco. She'll be all right."

Ollie saw her own reflection. And Brian's reflection. And the reflection of someone else. A woman.

But was it a reflection? The woman in the mirror was tapping on the glass.

Tap.

Tap.

"Olivia," whispered a voice in her ear, as though the person reflected in the mirror really were standing next to her. "Olivia, I'm here."

"Ollie, I don't like this," said Brian.

Was it her mother's voice? It might have been her mother's voice.

"Mom?" Ollie whispered. In the mirror, she could see curling dark hair like her own. She still couldn't make out a face.

But that voice in her ear said, "Olivia, come here. You're in danger, and we don't have much time."

Ollie went closer. The woman in the mirror put her hand flat against the glass, as though the mirror were a window and they were staring at each other through it. Brian stood rigid beside her. Ollie reached out, tentatively. She laid her shaking hand against the woman's. The glass was icy under her fingers.

"Mommy?" she whispered, her voice a hopeful, agonized thread. "What is it?"

At that moment, the firelight flared up behind her, flared up bright, as though someone had thrown three logs on the sullen, smoldering blaze. Brian cried, "Ollie, Ollie!" But he seemed suddenly very far away.

The light brightened as the fire leaped up. It fell on the woman's face.

She was blue-lipped and black-nosed. She wore a black dress and a black veil over her hair. When she smiled at Ollie, her teeth were sharp.

It was the woman from the hallway.

The woman from her nightmares.

Ollie tried to yank away, but black-nailed fingers had curled *out* of the mirror glass, catching her hand and holding it. "Got you," breathed Mother Hemlock.

The warning from her dream raced through Ollie's

shocked and panicking brain: Stay out of closets and *don't look in the mirror.*

Should have taken the advice. Ollie wanted to scream with terror and disappointment. *Mom, where are you?* She struggled to throw the woman off. There was a commotion behind her, but Ollie couldn't tell what was going on. All of her skin felt cold and heavy with fear.

Mother Hemlock yanked Ollie forward hard enough to wrench her face-first into the mirror. Ollie screamed, and her free arm flew up to protect her head against smashing into the glass.

But she didn't smash into the glass. She was dragged forward and forward and forward some more, until she tumbled and fell flat on her face onto a foul-smelling carpet.

There was total silence. Total stillness. For a long second, Ollie lay still, hearing only her fast, frightened breathing. Then she dragged herself to her knees. "Dad?" she called, hearing her voice shake. "Coco? Brian?"

No answer.

10

OLLIE SCRAMBLED TO her feet. All was silent. The fire in front of her burned low and red. For a second, Ollie thought she had imagined falling forward, falling . . .

Falling through the mirror.

How could you fall through a mirror?

Then she realized that the air smelled different. It smelled like mold and damp and rotten food. It was freezing cold. She was shivering.

Next Ollie realized what wasn't there. There was a fire, but no blankets.

Rotten carpet, but no tables.

Herself, but no friends.

She was alone.

Ollie spun in a circle. She was in the dining hall. But

it had changed. This was the dining hall of her nightmare. The front window was broken and boarded up. Glass crunched when she moved.

"Coco?" Ollie whispered again. Then a little louder: "Brian? Dad?" Where were they? Where was she? She spun in another circle, trying desperately not to panic. She wasn't succeeding too well. "Mom?"

No one answered. But the sound of a soft laugh came from the mirror.

For the mirror was still there. One of the only things that was. It was hanging on the wall opposite the fireplace. But now Ollie couldn't see her own reflection in this mirror. Instead, she saw her friends moving around near the fire. Their lips moved as they called, *Ollie, Ollie.* But she couldn't hear them.

She *had* gone through the mirror, Ollie thought. She was alone. She'd never been so afraid.

Then, with a surge of relief, Ollie realized that Mr. Voland was standing right next to the mirror, looking into it, staring right at her. The light from the fire on Ollie's side of the glass fell on his face. "Mr. Voland!" Ollie called. "Mr. Voland!" She reached up and pressed her hands to the mirror's cold glass. It felt just like a mirror. Rigid. Unyielding. She couldn't get back through it. But if Mr. Voland could somehow hear her . . .

"No need to shout," Mr. Voland said calmly, as though he'd heard her thought. "I can hear you, Olivia."

Mr. Voland, Ollie wanted to say. *Help me.* But she didn't say it. Something about his slow, satisfied smile choked the words back down her throat. Instead she said, "Where am I?"

"Behind the mirror," he said. He was still smiling gently.

Behind him, Ollie glimpsed Coco frantically trying to shake her mother awake. But Ms. Zintner didn't wake up. Brian was trying to do the same thing to Ollie's dad.

He didn't wake up either.

Cold terror filled Ollie. She stared at Mr. Voland. He smiled back at her. "Is my dad okay?" she whispered.

"Just asleep," he said. "But he will not wake. Not tonight."

Ollie's mouth was completely, utterly dry. "You," she croaked, licked her lips, tried again. "Who are you?"

"I think you know," he said.

She did. She didn't want to. She didn't want it to be true. But it was, and she did. Stammering, Ollie said, "But you—you were different. The last time."

His smile was colder than the freezing lodge. "I never look the same twice," he said. "Where would the fun be in that?"

Now she recognized the smile. Ollie, if she lived to be

132

a hundred, could never forget that particular smile. How could she not have known? How could she not have recognized him the second he walked into the lodge?

But maybe he hadn't wanted her to recognize him. Maybe he knew how to hide somehow.

"You—" Ollie could barely bring herself to say it. "You're Seth. You're the smiling man."

Seth laughed, and it was Mr. Voland's warm, happy laugh. But then his smile widened until it wasn't a smile at all but a specter's gruesome grin, all teeth. "Discovered at last," he said. "I wondered how long it would take you."

Ollie slammed the side of her fist against the glass of the mirror. But it was completely solid under her hand, and she was on the wrong side of it. Mr. Voland—Seth—didn't even flinch. "No one outwits me, my girl," he went on. "And *you* didn't outwit me last time, mind you. You had *help*." He raised his hand. Something small and dark dangled limp between his fingers. It was her mother's watch. He'd taken it—when had he taken it? Ollie touched her wrist, felt the bare skin where her watch had been. She thought of reaching for the Ouija board in the dark, so distracted by the slide of the letters that she hadn't noticed . . .

"It was you!" Ollie snapped, realizing. "You stopped her from talking to me! You stopped my watch from working! She was saying BEWARE about *you*. You scared us,

133

you tricked us, you lied to us! The whole time, everything that's been happening here, it's been *you*."

Seth bowed to her in a theatrical and old-fashioned kind of acknowledgment. "Of course it was me. Well, except for Mother Hemlock. She's real enough." He grinned. "Such a helpful old thing, that hag. But mostly it was me."

Ollie slammed the side of her fist against the mirror again. "Give me my watch! Give it back! Give it *back*!"

"Not so fast, my girl," said Seth, coming close to the mirror, speaking low and fast and deadly earnest. "We are going to play our game again. The game of wits. The game you cheated at last time in the corn maze. With the help of this very watch." He held it up again between two fingers. "This time you won't have your cheat. And you have until dawn to find your way back through the mirror. If you don't find your way, well, then you'll stay right where you are."

She was silent, staring at him in horror.

Seth continued: "Your friends can try to help you if they choose, but if they help and you fail, then you *all* will be trapped on the other side of the mirror. However, if your friends lie back down and sleep like good little boys and girls, then they will wake up safe and sound with no memory of you at all, and everyone will go home safely."

Seth rubbed his hands together, looking absolutely delighted with his game. "What will they choose, what will they choose?" he singsonged.

Ollie could hardly speak around her dry throat and tongue. "And," she whispered. "And my dad? What will happen to him?"

Seth pursed his lips. "Oh," he said. "No grown-ups allowed in this game, my dear. The adults, all four of them, will sleep until dawn. If your friends play and you lose, then the grown-ups will wake up three children short with no idea what happened to you. So sad. Another tragedy in Hemlock Lodge." Seth wiped a theatrical tear from his eye. Ollie hated him like she'd never hated anyone in her entire life.

"However, if your friends go quietly to sleep," he continued, "then I will make sure that the adults forget all about you. Your father won't be in the least unhappy. You will just be his little dead daughter, who died along with his wife in a tragic plane crash. He will go home and marry Coco's mother. Your friend Coco will be his little daughter. He will live long and happily."

"And if I beat you?" Ollie asked, wishing her voice sounded strong and fierce instead of being a thin, appalled croak.

A lifted brow from Seth. "You won't beat me," he said

gently. "It's not *impossible*, mind you; it wouldn't be a game if winning were impossible. Highly unlikely, however. Of course, should the unlikely happen, your prize is to be restored to the lodge, storm over, the watch on your wrist, your friends with you, all safe and sound. It won't happen. But that is the prize. In the meantime, I can be generous. You may have one minute to talk to your friends. Say good-bye and all. Convince them not to help you, lest they be trapped there with you. Then—let the game begin." His smile was wide and joyous, the way a wolf grins, pouncing. With a neat dramatic gesture, he fastened Ollie's watch to his own wrist. "May the best of us win."

Ollie, shocked, afraid, wanted to scream at him in fury and terror, to slam her fist on the mirror again. But she held herself very still and breathed. In, out.

Ollie's mom had taken her to do scary things all the time when Ollie was little. Climbing huge trees. Climbing boulders. Jumping off rocks into deep water. *Olivia,* she would say, *when you're scared, it means you're thinking of the future. You're thinking of what might happen. If you're doing something risky, you can't think of the future. You must only think of now. And if you only think of now, then you won't be scared.*

But, little Ollie had said, *I don't know how to only think of now.*

Breathe, her mother had said. *Breathing is what you're doing right now. So breathe. Think of that and nothing else.*

So Ollie breathed, and thought of that and nothing else, and so she didn't cry when Brian and Coco ran up to the mirror like they'd been shot from a cannon. As though Seth had been holding them back somehow. She didn't know what Seth could do, Ollie realized. She didn't know anything about him. After they'd made it home safely the last time, she'd tried to forget the smiling man altogether.

It had never occurred to her that he might not forget them.

Ollie couldn't see her friends' faces very well, since there was only the weak glow of the fire to illuminate them. But Ollie didn't need to see their faces well. She knew them by heart. They were closer than a brother and sister would have been. They were her best friends.

Brian and Coco were both trying to talk at once. But Ollie put a hand up. They went quiet. *Breathe.* Ollie felt strangely calm now.

"Mr. Voland is the smiling man," said Ollie. "He found us; he's come back." She could see him just at the edge of the mirror, watching them. He could probably hear everything they were saying.

Her friends stared at her. Coco's mouth and eyes were round and ridiculous with horror.

"He says I'm stuck here," said Ollie, talking fast, trying not to think too hard about what she was saying. "Unless I find the way back through the mirror before dawn." Ollie put her palms on the mirror to illustrate. "But I don't know how to do that. He says you can help me, but if we fail, then you'll be trapped on this side of the mirror too. So—" Ollie swallowed hard. "Better you don't help me. If you go to bed, and sleep, it'll be okay in the morning."

Brian said, "Owl, don't be an idiot. We're going to help you."

"But you *can't*!" Ollie snapped, and lost her fragile control over herself. She pressed her hands desperately against the glass. "Brian—Coco—our parents—my dad—they can't lose you too. Better one of us than all three of us."

"Ollie," said Coco, "Brian's right. We're not leaving you. And—why do you believe that guy, anyway? He's the smiling man? He's a big huge liar! He lied about being Mr. Voland. He's probably been lying this whole time about Mount Hemlock, about ghosts, about all of it. Maybe he's lying about this too. We're going to help you. Hang on, okay? Just hang on. We'll get you out." Coco put both her tiny hands on the glass, right against Ollie's on the other side. But Ollie couldn't feel it. There was a mirror between them. Coco's eyes were huge and shining with intensity now. "It'll be all right, Ollie. It will."

"I love you," said Ollie to her friends, just as their eyes widened. Coco and Brian both started to shout a warning. Ollie didn't hear it, though. She stopped hearing sound through the mirror a second before a gray bony hand fell on her shoulder.

"Got you!" said a low, dead voice, right in her ear. "Bad girl, talking out of turn. It's the closet for you until you learn some manners."

11

COCO SAW THE gray-faced woman sneaking up behind Ollie, and she screamed a warning. She saw Ollie's lips move, asking *what*, but Coco didn't hear anything. It was like a movie that had suddenly been muted. Brian was pounding his fists on the glass. "Ollie!" he was shouting. "Ollie!"

Coco had a swift, horrible glimpse of the woman digging her bony fingers into Ollie's arm, wrenching her around, and dragging her friend, struggling, across the dining room. Coco could see Ollie's mouth move as she yelled. Brian was still banging on the glass, as though he could force a way through. But Coco didn't think they could.

Coco then did one of the biggest, hardest things she'd ever done in her whole life. She turned away from the mirror. She turned away from the sight of her best friend being hauled away somewhere she and Brian couldn't follow. She pressed her lips together. She pressed her hands to her sides so they wouldn't shake. She couldn't help Ollie by shouting. She could help her by figuring out what was going on.

Coco marched right across the dining room and stopped in front of Mr. Voland—Seth—the smiling man. He was beside the fireplace, watching the scene in the mirror opposite, laughing with such giddy delight that he'd sunk down on a chair. When he looked up at her, he had to wipe actual tears of laughter from his eyes.

"Well?" he asked her, still snorting.

Coco didn't say anything for a moment. She was swallowing the urge to scream at him, or to beg like a little kid for him to bring Ollie back. She knew that wouldn't help. Instead she tried to think.

Coco hadn't actually met the smiling man in the corn maze, the way Ollie had. Ollie had confronted him on the platform in the middle of the corn maze, in the world behind the mist. But Coco and Brian hadn't seen her do it. They'd been on the ground, held by scarecrows. The only things Coco knew about the smiling man came from what Ollie had told her about that night. And from reading an old book called *Small Spaces*.

So Coco didn't know very much about him. She'd

imagined him, of course, and she'd seen him in her nightmares. But her imagination had supplied a cloud of bats around the smiling man's head, smoke coming out of his nostrils, snakes wrapped around his wrists, and his smile the empty grin of a skull. Her nightmares had given him a thin, nasty voice and a face always in shadow.

But in real life, the smiling man wasn't like that at all. He still looked a little like plain Mr. Voland, with freckles across his nose. But now his smile was cruel and happy and wild, and his light-and-dark eyes seemed to take over the rest of his face. Looking at him, Coco wondered how she'd ever thought even for a second that he was just an ordinary person.

She took a deep breath. She saw that Mr. Voland— Seth—had taken Ollie's watch. He was wearing it on his own wrist. Coco felt faintly sick, seeing it there. Her mind raced.

She said slowly, "So you are the smiling man. You had blond hair before."

"What's a face?" remarked Seth. "Just another kind of deception."

"Did you come back here just to trap Ollie behind the mirror?"

"Yes," he said. "For she beat me once. And I do not like to lose." He gave her a flicker of a smile. She really hated that smile. Behind her, Brian had stopped shouting and thumping on the mirror. There was the swish of his feet in socks on the floor as he came up beside Coco. A sideways glance showed her the shine of furious tears on Brian's face.

"Ollie said there was a way for her to get back to this side of the mirror," Coco went on, choosing her words, trying to *think*. "If she can find it."

"There is a way," said Seth. "But she won't find it."

"She will. We're going to help her," said Coco.

Seth's smile widened. "I hoped you would. I'll have all three of you behind the mirror, in the end."

At that, Brian, with a yell and a flying tackle worthy of the high school football team, threw himself at the smiling man.

But he missed. Seth didn't even move, just sat in his chair, as cool as the winter night outside, and somehow Brian was left to slam face-first into the table behind him.

"Brian!" Coco cried, and ran over to haul him upright. "That was dumb," she told him. His lip was split and bleeding.

Brian just shook his head, wiped off his split lip, and said to Seth, fists clenched, "Bring her back!"

"No," said Seth calmly.

Coco wanted to give Brian a hug; she wanted to help

him calm down. She wanted to tell him, *This isn't a hockey game; it isn't a duel in the fantasy books you like to read. You can't just be the fastest, the strongest, and the bravest and win. We have to make a plan.*

Coco might have been tiny, but she was good at making plans. She'd played enough chess. At least, she hoped she had. She was still thinking as hard as she could. Seth had taken Ollie's watch. It must be important. Possibly they wouldn't be able to figure out how to get through the mirror without the watch's help. They needed the watch. But how to get it back?

I like games, Mr. Voland had said. He was playing one now. A nasty game. One that only he understood. But what if Coco challenged him to a different game?

Seth leaned back in his chair, still smiling. He was enjoying himself, she realized. He wasn't worried about them outsmarting him. Maybe he was overconfident.

She licked her lips. Brian looked like he was about to start shouting again. So she spoke first. "That watch isn't yours," Coco said to Seth. She was surprised at how strong her voice sounded. Not thin or squeaky at all. "It's Ollie's. Give it back."

"It's mine now," said Seth. "I take it you mean to help your friend and be trapped alongside her? Very well. Go help her. You are wasting time."

"Not without Ollie's watch, we aren't," Coco said.

"I fail to see how you'll get it," said Seth. "I'm not giving it to you."

Coco swallowed hard. "I'll play you for it," she said. "Unless you're scared of a kid outsmarting you. You said you like games." Beside her, she felt Brian's stare, but he didn't say anything.

Seth snorted. "Wiser and greater men than you have tried *outsmarting* me, as you put it. They are dead now."

"Well," said Coco very coldly, "that's too bad for them. But *I'm* a girl, and I bet I can beat you at chess." She hadn't forgotten him cheerfully mocking her and Ollie earlier. She hadn't been playing very seriously then. Maybe he'd decided she was terrible. She hoped he had.

She hoped she wasn't.

Seth went still. His eyes narrowed. Coco's mouth was dry, and she was shaking with the coldest terror she'd ever felt in her whole life. "Unless you're scared you'll lose," she added.

Seth just raised a casual eyebrow. "The last time I played chess was with a knight by the sea, and his life was the forfeit."

"Great," said Coco. "You know how to play, then."

His laugh was unpleasant. "Yes," he said. "I know how to play. And I accept. One match. The watch is yours if you win, for all the good it will do you. But what will you give me if you lose?"

He snorted when Coco didn't say anything. She couldn't quite bring herself, like the knight by the sea, to offer her life. "I thought so," he said. "I will not play if you do not also have a forfeit."

"Me," said Brian.

Coco whirled. "Brian, *what*?"

Brian gave her a small, shaky smile. "If she loses, I'll go back behind the mirror with Ollie," he said. "I'll even promise to stay there forever. 'Cause, you see, Coco won't lose."

"Well enough," said Seth. "I accept."

"Brian, that is the worst idea I have ever heard," said Coco.

"I've seen you play enough times," said Brian. "I trust you. Got a better idea, Tiny?" She glared at him by reflex, and it made her feel better. More normal. She realized Brian had called her that on purpose, to annoy her so she wouldn't be scared.

"Okay," said Coco, and hoped she hadn't just decided to do something amazingly stupid. "I'll get my chess set."

"No need," said Seth, and pointed at the table in front of him.

A chessboard was already set up there, its pieces made of perfect, hard, glossy stone, black and white.

Brian let out a low whistle. "You got this, Coco," he said. "Just like in *Harry Potter*."

"I never read it," said Coco, between gritted teeth. "But if I win and we get out of this, you are never going to call me Tiny ever again."

"I wouldn't do that anyway," said Brian seriously. "And I'm really sorry I kept calling you that."

"It's okay," said Coco. "I'm getting a growth spurt, though. One of these days."

They smiled at each other; forced smiles, but better than nothing.

Seth cracked his fingers. The fire set points of red light into his eyes. "Let us play."

———

Mother Hemlock—at least Ollie thought the gray woman was Mother Hemlock—might have been a ghost. Or she might not have been. How did you tell? Ollie realized how little—how very little she knew about ghosts. Or anything. She and Brian and Coco had come out of the world behind the mist only wanting to forget about it. To go back to school, be normal kids, ride their bikes, do their homework, make scones in the Egg with her dad.

Ollie hadn't even considered that maybe they'd been

making a mistake. That even if they were done with the world behind the mist, it wasn't done with them.

She wasn't behind the mist now. She was behind a mirror, and the gray woman was hauling her across the dining room, muttering gleefully.

"Upstairs! Upstairs *now*! To the closet first! And then straight to bed with you, missy! No supper! I'll teach you to disobey! I'll *teach you*."

Ollie fought. "I didn't—disobey—let go of me!" She thrashed in the thing's grip, head-butted her, bit her horrible-tasting arm, let her legs go limp so that she was dragged across the floor. It was like being a toddler; the woman—the ghost—didn't even react. Ollie felt panic starting to choke her. If she could not get free . . .

Another dark shape was waiting for them in the archway between the dining room and the lobby. It wore a blue jacket and a ski mask. Ollie couldn't see very well. The only light in the room was the dull, hellish glow of the fire, the only thing that was the same on both sides of the mirror. His hands hung down by his sides, and he wasn't wearing gloves. The fingers were black. *Not ash*, Ollie realized. *Frostbite.*

Was this Gabriel Bouvier? she wondered.

Or Gabriel Bouvier's ghost?

He made a horrible garbled sound and raised his hand, palm out. Like he was saying *STOP*.

Mother Hemlock slowed a little. "I've been kind," she snapped at him, in a voice like old bones crunching. "I've given you houseroom here, traveler. But this is still my house. *Get out of my way.*" And she raised a hand in return, pointing a finger directly at him. The ghost in the ski mask stumbled backward like she'd hit him, even though she hadn't even touched him.

But to raise her hand and point, Mother Hemlock had to let go of Ollie's arm. They were close to the fireplace. Close enough for Ollie to pull her hand into the sleeve of her jacket, lunge at the hearth with all her strength, and grab a fistful of hot coals. She shoved them up at Mother Hemlock's grayish, furious face.

Mother Hemlock fell back, smoldering, screeching. She wiped embers from her eyes. "That was foolish," she said, in the coldest voice Ollie had ever heard.

But Ollie didn't wait around to find out why it was foolish. She had bolted for the second archway, running for her life.

But something stood in the other archway too.

It was the bear. The dead, stuffed bear. It was standing on its hind legs, upright on its wooden stand. Blocking her way.

Ollie slowed. The bear's mouth was open. Huge white teeth showed in a snarl. One stiff paw was upraised to strike.

149

And a sound was coming from it. A low, soft sound. She didn't recognize it at first. It was too strange. Then she understood. The dead bear was growling.

As Ollie watched, frozen, the dead bear fell to all fours. Licked its chops. Then, creaking, the dead bear charged.

Ollie slewed around, found Mother Hemlock *right behind her*, her mouth pinched down in rage, one sleeve of her dress smoldering. She snatched at Ollie again, but Ollie dodged her and raced back through the dining room. The footsteps of the dead bear sounded close behind her, and she could smell its reek: a combination of dust and formaldehyde.

Ollie, wild with panic, wove and dodged. The bear took a swipe at her; its claws snagged on the hem of her hoodie, and she heard fabric tear as she ran.

It got darker the farther away from the fire Ollie went. She stubbed her toes again and again, banged her shins on debris she couldn't see, snagged her socks on splinters, tried not to trip and fall. She was expecting every second to feel the bear's claws sinking into her skin.

A shrill cry from above was her only warning before, with a rush of wind and the reek of more embalming fluid, the talons of one of the dead eagles raked through her hair, cutting her scalp. Huge wings beat around her head, making her gag with their stink.

But by then Ollie had made it across the dining room. She fended off the bird, shoved open the kitchen door, and threw herself through. She was only a step ahead of the thudding stride of the bear and, worse, the clacking footsteps of Mother Hemlock.

Ollie slammed the door shut and put her back against it just as the door shuddered, like the dead bear had thrown all its weight at it. It was so dark that Ollie couldn't tell whether her eyes were open or shut. The door shuddered again. *Light,* Ollie thought. *I need light.*

In a flash, Ollie remembered the matches. She was still wearing her hoodie. She plunged her hand into the front pocket and retrieved the matchbook, a slim, crisp shape against her fingers. Her hand was shaking. *Breathe, Olivia,* said the memory of her mother's voice, somewhere in the back of her brain. *Breathe.*

She knew that if she managed to drop that book of matches, send it skittering across the floor, then in that ferocious darkness, she'd never find it again.

The kitchen door shook. Ollie leaned against it with all her weight. But she knew it couldn't last. She was tall and broad-shouldered and strong for her age, but she was *still* just an eleven-year-old girl.

Gritting her teeth and working by touch, Ollie pulled out a match and found the rough side of the matchbook with the pad of her thumb. She hadn't thought about the cold since she came through the mirror. There had been a lot else on her mind. But now she realized, by the sheer difficulty she was having using her fingers on the matches, that it was cold and getting colder.

Ollie thought of the ghosts' frostbitten hands, and she shuddered, almost dropping her matchbook. *That won't happen to me,* she promised herself. *It won't.*

She took one more deep breath and struck a match.

In the flash of its light, she had a swift glimpse of the lodge kitchen. It wasn't the shiny, modern kitchen that her dad had made pancakes in that morning. Instead she saw wooden countertops and dusty pots; it looked like a museum kitchen, smelling of old food and rot and dust all at once.

Her match was already flickering.

She turned it back and forth, hunting for a door, praying there was one.

She saw a face.

And froze.

She wasn't alone in the kitchen.

A little girl, wearing a long white nightgown, stood in the middle of the kitchen. She was staring straight at Ollie with her frozen-open eyes.

She was pointing. The match was about to burn Ollie's fingers, but she followed the direction of the ghost's finger.

Saw a cabinet, a little open.

The match went out again, leaving Ollie trembling, and not alone in the dark.

She threw herself at the remembered direction of the open cabinet door, scrabbled, and managed to drag herself inside, hiding just as the kitchen door burst open.

A growl came from the doorway. She heard a sniff. Ollie hadn't been able to get the cabinet door closed all the way. Her frantic heartbeat seemed to rock her body back and forth. She just hoped they couldn't hear it.

She kept perfectly still.

The bear growled again. Its claws scraped on the floor. It crossed the kitchen. Then Ollie heard the cold voice of Mother Hemlock. "Well, where did she go, the little rat? Down the stairs? Or—is she hiding?"

The dead bear's clawed feet halted. Ollie, with a shaking hand, groped in the empty cabinet, looking for something, anything, that she could use.

A flat piece of ceramic met her frantically groping hand. Plate? Saucer? She didn't care. She picked it up and hurled it out of the cabinet, hard, so that it flew across the room and smashed into the opposite wall.

The bear roared, and she heard its claws scrabbling—scrabbling *away*, like a dog, as it followed the sound. In that second, Ollie flung herself out of the cabinet, across the kitchen, and darted silently through the skinny door on the opposite wall. The door that led into the basement.

She found herself sprinting down a dark stairwell, leading into blackness.

12

SETH ENDED UP playing the white side, like some kind of really bad joke. Maybe he had a sense of humor. He probably did, Coco decided. He'd laughed hard enough at tricking Ollie through the mirror. She tried not to think about the things the smiling man would find funny.

Each chess piece, white and black, was laid out neatly in its place. Coco ran her fingertips over her ranks of black pawns and knights and bishops, feeling them icy under her hand. Part of her wondered where the chessboard came from. *I didn't see it. And then I did. Is that magic? Is there such a thing as magic?*

She didn't know. There was too much she didn't know. Suddenly she was desperate to win, if only to be able to get out, to go back, to find a library, and to learn everything she wished she knew.

She wished she knew how good Seth was at chess. There was a chance he'd be way better than her, that he'd know impossible combinations, that she'd be checkmated in five moves. If that happened, then Brian would pay the price.

Don't think about that, she ordered herself.

Coco was good. She knew that. But she wasn't— whatever the smiling man was—old and mean and clever. And so, she was afraid. She licked her lips, wiped her sweating palms one more time. White always goes first. Seth moved his queen's pawn, sat back and smiled at Coco.

Here goes, she told herself. Clenching her free hand, she made her first move. To her surprise, her hand didn't shake.

He *was* good. Really good, even. But the opening gambits became the middle of the game, and they were still trading pieces. Coco was still playing. She wasn't beaten. Slowly, the smile fell off his face.

They played in silence, fast, and it was the hardest chess game that Coco had ever played in her life. For one, there were a lot of things she had to force herself not to think about. She couldn't wonder if Ollie was all right, for example. She couldn't wonder what would happen to her mom and Ollie's dad if they woke up the next morning and Ollie, Brian, and Coco were all gone.

Coco couldn't even look up and meet the eyes of the player across from her, because every time she did, her courage shriveled up to nothing. Every time he moved his hand, she saw the two forefingers, thin, spidery, the exact same length, a reminder that he was older than her, nastier than her, that he was enjoying himself. It was all actually a game to him. But it wasn't to Coco.

So she stopped looking at his hands. She only watched the pieces as he moved them. She pretended she was back in school, playing Ollie again in the middle school chess championship. She imagined it so hard that she could almost smell the cider and marker smell of Mr. Easton's classroom.

The battle raged across the board. They traded pieces. She set traps, and he evaded them; he set traps for *her* that she barely saw in time. Finally, they were at the endgame, still matched, and finally Coco advanced her queen, took a deep breath, then advanced her pawn.

This is it. Please, she thought. *Oh, please.* She heard Brian beside her make a soft sound of protest, seeing the move she'd made. But Coco didn't even look at him.

Seth captured her queen, sat back, and grinned at her. "So much for that," he said.

Coco didn't answer. Instead she advanced another pawn. "Check," she said.

"Last defiance?" he asked, moving his king out of danger. Out of the corner of her eye, Coco could see Brian clenching his hands so hard the nails were actually cutting into his palms.

"Check," Coco said again, doggedly, moving her bishop, and this time Seth actually frowned, and, while Coco held her breath, he put his queen in between his king and her threatening bishop. And Coco let out a quavering breath, moved her knight, and said, "Checkmate."

Brian put his head in his hands. He said a couple of very bad words. Then he said, "Coco, that was amazing."

Coco said, "Thanks." Her eyes were still on the person across the table.

Seth's hands had gone still. A thick, ominous quiet hung over Hemlock Lodge. He stared at the board. He stared at Coco. This time she dared meet the faint red gleam in the dark of his eyes. She found herself asking, ridiculously, "Did *he* win? The knight by the sea?"

"He lost," said Seth. He stared at her a minute more.

And then he laughed, a high, terrifying sound, and Coco said, "Stop it!"

"Why?" he asked, still chortling. "The last time I was so excellently entertained, there was plague in Europe." But he did not look entertained. He looked angry.

Coco said, "You're horrible and you lost. You lost. Give me Ollie's watch."

He didn't do anything. Coco shot to her feet. "You promised!"

He got to his feet too then. "I did promise," he said. "There is a way to win, but you won't find it. Not even with this thing." But he didn't move to take off the watch.

"We'll take our chances," said Coco. She waited.

Slowly, Seth unfastened the watch from his wrist. His green eye flashed.

Coco understood what he was going to do about half a second before he dropped the watch into her waiting hands. He had promised to give her the watch if she won. He *hadn't* promised not to do anything nasty afterward.

Without giving herself time to think, Coco reached out and snatched the watch from Seth's grip; with her other hand, she reached down and scooped up the Ouija board and planchette, knocking over chess pieces left and right. "Run!" she snapped at Brian. "Run!"

She pelted through the archway into the lobby, not looking to see if Brian was following her. Of course, he was. Brian was leading the whole school district in hockey assists that season. Brian was a *team player*, as their PE teacher liked to say. And he'd been watching her the whole time. Trusting her. Waiting for Coco to make the play.

Even though she was sprinting out of breath across the lobby, Coco felt a little flicker of pride. She'd made the play, all right.

They flew toward the stairs on the opposite side of the lobby. Brian was way faster than her, but he kept his steps even with hers and they hit the stairs side by side. Then Brian slowed down a little, looking up. "You sure, Coco?" he asked. The darkness in the hallway was thick. "We don't know what's up there."

"Nope," she said. "We don't." But she kept on running up the stairs. She hated to do it. She could see that Brian did too. They were leaving her mom and Ollie's dad just lying there *asleep*, defenseless.

But Seth had said the game wasn't about their parents. Coco believed that. She had to believe that. Because they couldn't save Ollie *and* stand watch over the sleeping adults. They needed to get away from Seth and his tricks. They needed to go somewhere private and figure out what to do. Make a plan.

So Coco ran up the stairs, into the darkness, and Brian went with her.

"Why'd you grab the Ouija board?" Brian was taking the steps two at a time, bounding as he talked.

"Because," said Coco, panting. The Ouija board was awkward under her arm. "I saw it in the mirror."

"So?" said Brian.

"I saw the board in the mirror. It was *reflected* in the mirror. In—wherever Ollie was. Nothing else was. Not me or you or Seth or anything. Not the blankets. But the Ouija board was there. I could see it on the floor behind Ollie. That seemed weird. So I grabbed it."

Brian nodded. He took it from her. "I'll carry it. You're clumsy enough without trying to carry anything."

He wasn't being mean, just practical, Coco knew. They didn't need her tripping over her own feet on top of everything else. "Thanks," she said.

"Don't mention it." He didn't call her Tiny. Coco felt that surge of pride again.

They were halfway up the stairs when she risked a quick look behind them. She didn't see any sign of Seth. No, the lobby was totally empty and silent. The dead animals were glassy-eyed in the firelight.

Somehow the silence was worse than any noise.

"Brian," said Coco, frowning. "The black bear is gone."

Brian had stopped when she did; now he scanned the lobby in turn. "So are the coyotes," he said. His voice had gone flat and tense.

Coco looked hard, squinting in the dark. Brian was right.

He licked his lips. "You know, Coco, if scarecrows can come to life after dark—"

A long, low snarl sounded through the lobby. Then another. Strange dry growls. A little like a dog, but choked, somehow. Like its vocal cords didn't work right.

Coco heard nails clicking, like dogs crossing a kitchen

floor. The sounds were coming closer. There was a chorus of growls. The shadows in the lobby were moving.

"The coyotes," Brian whispered. "They're *coming*. Coco, Come on!"

He pulled her around and up the stairs just as howls broke out from every part of the lobby and the shadows seemed, all at once, to leap for the stairwell.

Brian and Coco bolted up into the darkness.

Below them, they heard a bark, and an answering howl. There was a louder clatter of dog nails as dead paws slipped on the lobby floor. Coco risked another look back; she heard the coyotes' panting breaths, but didn't see anything, and that was the worst of all.

They were at the top of the stairs. The hallway stretched on into the dimness. But, strangely, unlike the lobby and dining room, there *were* electric lights on up there. The wall lamps were lit. But they weren't glowing a nice yellow now. Just a faint green. They cast puddles of sickly light, in between stripes of darkness on the carpet. Both Brian and Coco hesitated at the top of the stairs. But then the growling came again, closing in behind them. They heard the padding of feet on the stairwell, the odd creak of formaldehyde-stuffed limbs.

Coco glanced behind. Still didn't see anything. "Brian—" she began.

But he'd already grabbed her hand, pulling her along,

and was fleeing again. "We have to stay ahead of them!" he said.

"Brian!" Coco tried again, even as she ran alongside him. She was panting; Brian was in a lot better shape than she was. He let go of her hand; she tried to keep up. But he was faster than her. He got a step ahead. Then another. Then Coco did trip on the carpet, went sprawling, and got rug burn on her hands as she fell.

From the ground, Coco cried out, "Brian, Brian!"

No answer. He couldn't have gotten that far ahead! Coco scrabbled to her feet, turned around—but there were no coyotes.

No one and nothing but her.

Complete silence in the hallway. She couldn't see Brian at all. Coco began to hurry along the corridor, following Brian, calling his name.

But no one answered.

After a few steps, something caught her foot and she tripped again.

What had tripped her this time? Coco groped around on the floor. It was the Ouija board. "Brian?" she whispered. She gathered up the Ouija board. The planchette was still in her pocket.

There was still no sign of Brian. Nor of the coyotes. The hallway was empty.

Seth didn't actually come up the stairs after us, Coco

thought. *But that doesn't mean he's not trying to stop us. Maybe he sent the coyotes. Or at least made us think there were coyotes. To scare us. To separate us.*

"Brian!" she called again.

Silence. Coco was totally alone in the hallway. Eerie greenish lights burned every few feet. Between them were puddles of darkness.

Right next to her, a door rattled.

Coco jerked away. *Not this time,* she thought. *I'm not getting distracted by spooky doors this time.* She was about to hurry down the hall, looking for Brian, when a familiar voice spoke.

It came from behind the door.

"Coco!" it cried. "I'm in here! Let me out!"

Brian. It was *definitely* Brian's voice. Coco halted, rigidly listening. The door rattled again. "It's locked," said Brian. *"Coco, help me!"*

How could Brian have gotten into the closet? She reached a trembling hand toward the door handle, just as, a few feet farther down the hall, *another* door rattled. "Hey!" cried Brian's voice from the door ahead. "Hey, let me out! Ollie? Coco? Coco! Are you there?"

Now both doors were rattling together. Brian's voice came from *both* of them. He sounded desperate. "Please! Please. It's *so dark*. Coco. I don't know what to do. Let me out! Let me out!" There was a crash, like someone had banged both fists on the door.

Now a third door was rattling, farther down. And a fourth.

Coco realized with horror that every door along that whole endless hall was rattling, and her friend's voice was shouting from *all* of them, "Coco, let me out. *Let me out!*"

Coco stood there trembling, fighting the urge to clamp her hands over her ears. They couldn't all be Brian! But they all sounded like Brian. Were any of them Brian? The courage that had kept her hands steady while she played chess with Seth had totally deserted her. Her mind ran in circles. Was Brian in any of these closets? Or none of the closets? How many closets were there?

Were there really undead coyotes?

She had a terrible suspicion, almost a certainty, that somewhere in the shadows, the smiling man was watching, laughing while he and Coco played this stupid game in the hallway, as Ollie's time ran out and Brian disappeared forever into the depths of the lodge.

Calm down, Coco, she tried to tell herself. *Think. Think.* But she couldn't think, not with Brian's desperate voice echoing in her ears, shouting her name.

Move, she told herself. *You have to move.*

She went to the nearest rattling door.

"Brian?" Coco said. "How do I know it's you?"

"Tiny, of course it's me!" cried his voice from behind the door. The door handle shook harder than ever. "It's so dark in here. *Help me.*"

Brian had said he wouldn't call her Tiny again. Maybe that was a clue? That it wasn't the real Brian? Should she just start trying doors? Asking trick questions to whoever was in there? But there were dozens of doors in the hallway. How long would it take her? And what would happen to Ollie if she took all this time trying to find Brian?

As she stood there, indecisive, on the edge of panic, Coco heard a very soft beeping. Coming from her pocket. Where she'd shoved Ollie's watch in the race to get away. Coco, with a sudden surge of hope, pulled out Ollie's watch and looked at it.

Nothing. The watch display was blank. Some help there. Maybe she'd been wrong to waste so much time on the chess game to get Ollie's watch away from Seth.

Coco was about to put it back in her pocket. But then she paused, staring at the watch. It was still beeping. Why would it be beeping?

Coco licked her lips. She whispered, "If you can hear me, be quiet."

The watch fell silent. Coco let out a soft breath. Even

if Seth had somehow blocked the screen from working, maybe—

The doors in the hallway rattled louder than ever, and Brian's voice rose to a terrified scream. "Coco, Coco!"

Coco didn't let it distract her. She whispered to the watch. "One beep is no, and two beeps is yes. Beep three times right now if you understand me."

The watch was silent. Coco held her breath. Then, slowly, the watch beeped three times.

Coco let her breath out with a shudder. Then she had another terrible thought. What if *this* was a trick too? What if the beeping wasn't Ollie's mom, but Seth? She thought quickly.

"Ollie plays softball, yes or no?"

Two beeps. YES.

"Ollie is scared of dogs."

One beep. NO.

"Her favorite color is blue."

NO. True. Ollie's favorite color was yellow.

Okay. It definitely wasn't a foolproof test, but she needed *some* help and this seemed like the best Coco would get. She hitched Seth's Ouija board more firmly under her arm. She gathered her courage. "Okay," she said. "I need to find Brian. Which room is he in?"

She turned to the first door. "This one?"

The door she was pointing at shook back and forth. Brian's hopeless yell from inside hurt her ears.

But the watch beeped once. NO.

Coco began making her slow and steady way down the darkened hallway, crossing and recrossing to each door. Brian's voice yelled at her from all of them. Each time, she whispered, "Here?" and each time, the watch said NO.

Now Brian sounded mad. "Coco, are you playing or what? Coco, help! Coco, why do you hate me? *Coco*. Tiny, what's your problem? I never liked you anyway. You're so lame. Ollie's better than you, and braver than you and—"

On and on Brian's voice went, saying hurtful things, desperate things.

Coco closed her ears and kept going. The hallway seemed endless. At each door, the watch said NO, and NO. Coco's heart pounded. How much time had gone by? How much time did she have? She began to think that she'd just be walking until dawn, checking door after door, and then the sun would rise, and she'd be stuck in the smiling man's hallway forever. Maybe she'd been tricked anyway. Maybe the watch wasn't Ollie's mom at all.

Just then the watch began beeping urgently. Coco halted. Realized that she was right about in the middle of the hallway. As though she hadn't been walking for the last ten minutes.

Maybe she hadn't. She didn't know what was a trick

and what was real. All around, Brian's voice shouted at her. Was she alone in the dark? Did she have a friend behind *any* of the doors? Where was Ollie? Was the smiling man lurking in the shadows, watching her and laughing?

The watch was beeping softly. Not a YES or NO, but as though it were trying to talk to her. As though to tell her, *Calm down and look.*

Calm down, Coco thought. *Calm down.* She was surrounded by rattling doors. *That's the trick,* she thought. *He's full of tricks. He makes things seem different than they are. Don't listen.*

Then she realized that the door in front of her wasn't rattling at all. It was totally silent. "This one?" she whispered.

Two beeps.

Coco hesitated. She knew she either had to trust the watch or not, but she could imagine all kinds of horrible things lurking behind those doors.

But she gathered her courage, took the door by the handle, and pushed.

It wasn't a closet at all. It was a staircase. Coco, not expecting it, almost fell down the stairs. Gasping, she caught herself at the last second and peered in.

All the rattling closet doors had fallen silent. Brian's voice was silent too. In front of her, a simple flight of creaky wooden steps led down into darkness.

Coco absolutely did not want to go down those stairs by herself. She wanted to run back to her mom, wake her up, and ask what to do. She wanted to go to sleep in a warm bunk bed and have this all have been a dream when she woke up. She wanted Ollie and Brian with her.

But she'd lost Ollie and Brian. And she wouldn't get them back unless she was brave. She had to be brave.

"Do I go down there?" Coco whispered to the watch.

The watch beeped twice. YES.

Coco, sick with fright, thought of her friends waiting for her and gathered her courage. She hitched the Ouija board more firmly under her arm and went through and down.

Just as she went, somewhere out of sight, the bird clock whistled.

Coco prayed she had enough time.

13

OLLIE SPRINTED DOWN the stairs, hating the dark. Somewhere below her, she thought she saw a faint golden light. It was all that kept her from tripping and falling headfirst down the stairs. But the light also scared her. She didn't know what had made it. She didn't know what was waiting for her at the bottom of the stairs. The wooden steps creaked and snagged threads on her wool socks as she ran.

About halfway down, she realized that there were no footsteps following her. Ollie slowed, and then she stopped.

Utter silence on the stairwell. Ollie tried to quiet her panic-fast breathing, her racing heart. She wondered if Mother Hemlock and the black bear weren't following because they didn't need to. Because all they had to do was stand guard at the door and Ollie would be trapped in the basement until it was too late. Had she just missed her last chance of getting out of this place?

Tears pricked her eyes. She swallowed them, tried to think. She wasn't done yet! Coco and Brian would be somewhere, trying to help. But they were on the other side of the mirror. She didn't know what they were doing. Or even what they *could* do.

Ollie looked back up at the faint shape of the door she'd come through. Go down? Go back up? How long until dawn? The golden light below flickered. Ollie didn't know what was down there.

But she knew what was waiting for her up in the lobby.

Ollie ran as quietly as she could down the stairs.

They ended sooner than she was prepared for. Ollie lurched from the last step onto the stone floor of a basement so fast that she went sprawling painfully to her knees. She wrenched herself to her feet and looked around.

The basement was massive. Cavernous. Ollie, eyes open wide in the dark, turned in a nervous circle and glimpsed all kinds of things. Big lockers with labels like SUMMER CLOTHES, WINTER CLOTHES, HISTORY BOOKS, NIGHT-GOWNS. There were old rusty tools and nails on the floor. She breathed the musty damp and slow decay. She took a few cautious steps farther in, watching where she put her feet.

The basement was utterly quiet. Utterly still.

Or—almost still. The light moved. It shone from behind a set of lockers. It flickered and steadied. Like a candle flame. But who could have lit the candle? Cautiously, straining her senses to hear and see, Ollie crept around the corner of the old lockers. She stopped short. The light came from an old-fashioned oil lamp. It burned by itself on a small, splintering table.

Ollie knew about oil lamps. They had a few in the Egg, for when the power went out. The hollow base was full of lamp oil; there would be a piece of cotton for a wick, threaded up into a hollow glass tube. If you lit the wick, it burned slowly and steadily. You could brighten and dim the light by adjusting the wick up and down.

But how had a lit oil lamp made it down there? In the dark basement, on that side of the mirror? Ollie hesitated, listening hard. She couldn't hear anything but the sound of her own footsteps.

She went closer, examined the lamp. It seemed ordinary. Except that it was in the oddest of places. Had a ghost lit it? Did ghosts have lamps here?

Or was it Seth?

Maybe the lamp didn't matter, Ollie thought. How was she going to get back through the mirror? After Alice went through the looking glass, all she had to do was wake up, and she was home. Ollie didn't think that would work this time. Back in October, she and Brian and Coco had made it home from the other side of the mist because Ollie had a book that existed in both worlds. But there was no mist and no books this time.

Ollie didn't know what to do.

Think, she ordered herself furiously. *Think!*

Well, she needed to get out of the basement first, Ollie decided. She couldn't get back through the mirror in a basement that, as far as she could see, didn't have any mirrors.

Cautiously, Ollie reached for the lamp. The light would come in handy. But before she touched it, Ollie thought she heard a creaking from the stairs above her. The bear? Mother Hemlock? Were they chasing her after all?

Thud. Thud. Definitely footsteps.

She had to hide, Ollie thought. Disoriented, she looked frantically around. The lamplight ruined her night vision, and the shadows were deceptive. And even if she did hide, would the dead bear be able to *smell* her?

Well, if it could, she couldn't help it now. Ollie ducked behind another bank of lockers, trying to get out of range of the lamplight.

For a second, she crouched alone in the shadows, panting.

Then a thin, high, whispering voice spoke out of the darkness.

"You shouldn't have come here," it said.

———

Coco stepped cautiously down a creaking flight of wooden steps. The Ouija board was clamped tight under one arm. "Brian?" she called, her voice small and fragile in the darkness. "Brian?"

No sound. No answer. Distantly she thought she heard a howl. The coyotes? Her heart beat faster. She really hoped that Brian was okay. The stairs were narrow and wooden. Splinters snagged on her socks. It was almost completely dark. Far below, a single yellowish light burned. It barely illuminated the stairwell. She had to go carefully so she wouldn't trip. She took a cautious step down. Another.

It was hard to make out the walls, because of the darkness. But she could, a little. Coco slowed, then stopped.

There was writing on the walls. A *lot* of writing.

coco, said the walls. coco coco coco, blurring the letters of her name over and over and over. Then u left me u forgot me I HATE U I HATE U.

Despite herself, Coco cowered back from the ugly words. Maybe Brian had been in one of those closets and she had just left him . . .

Wait, *was* it Brian's handwriting? Was it Ollie's? Coco swallowed hard. That was dumb. Why would either of them be writing on a stairwell? "It's a trick," she whispered. "A trick, a trick."

She didn't know what kind of tricks the smiling man could do. Another piece of knowledge she wished she had. She'd beaten him at chess, but he'd tricked her and Brian into separating, hadn't he? If it was him, making the hall endless and full of Brian's voice, making dead coyotes chase them, putting writing on the basement wall, then what else could he do?

Coco swallowed back fear. If she panicked now, she'd be like a climber on a cliff face, stuck in the middle, afraid to go up, afraid to descend.

She started down the stairs again. Down and down she went. The stairs seemed to go on forever.

Suddenly Coco felt a gust of icy air from above. Then she heard running footsteps come thundering down behind her.

Coco spun around, pressed herself against a wall, her heart in her mouth.

She didn't see anyone at all. But she still heard footsteps. She instinctively flattened herself to the wall, as close as she could. The footsteps ran straight past her and kept going down into the basement.

All went quiet once more. Coco stood frozen with indecision.

The watch beeped again. Coco had almost forgotten it in her terror.

She whispered, "Should I go down?"

Two beeps. YES.

She didn't want to go down. Maybe it was the smiling man after all, maybe he knew all about Ollie and that was who was making the watch beep. "Ollie hates Brussels sprouts, doesn't she?" Coco whispered.

One beep. NO. That was true. Ollie loved Brussels sprouts, the weirdo.

Okay, then, Coco thought. As proof, maybe it was still kind of weak. Maybe it was the smiling man's lucky guess, but she had to trust it. Coco kept on padding down the stairs.

Finally she stepped off the stairs and onto a concrete floor and found herself in a gigantic space. Utterly still and utterly dark, except for a flickering light. Coco went around a pile of old clothes and saw a single oil lamp burning. It was just like the oil lamps that Ollie's dad had in the Egg. Coco stared at it. Where had that come from? Who had lit it? She scanned the basement. Complete and horrible silence.

The lamp illuminated dusty lockers and piles of boxes. Rusting tools.

Coco considered the lamp, thinking hard. Coco had taken the Ouija board because it was the only thing visible on both sides of the dining room mirror, after Ollie had gone through it.

But that wasn't completely true. Coco remembered suddenly that there had been another thing visible on both sides of the mirror.

The fire itself.

Okay, but so? She didn't know what that meant, or if it would be any help. It was only that the Ouija board was the first thing Coco had seen that had struck her as—different. Out of place. This lamp was the second.

She was reaching out a hand to pick up the lamp when she heard soft, skittering footsteps again. She still couldn't see anyone. "Brian?" she whispered. "Brian?"

No answer.

But Ollie's watch began to beep, loudly and steadily, in the darkness.

———

Ollie, crouching behind the lockers, froze when she heard the thin, whispering voice. *You shouldn't have come here.* It seemed to have spoken *right beside her*.

Very slowly, Ollie turned.

It was the ghost girl. Gretel, if that was her real name.

The ghost girl had been scary at a distance. She was worse close up. Her nose was black, as were the tips of her fingers. There were black specks on her cheeks. The rest of her was bloodless-white, her lips bluish. Her eyes were wide and unblinking.

"I tried to warn you," she whispered. "I tried. Too late. You're here and she's hunting you. Go away. I'm hiding. If she finds you, she'll find me."

It took Ollie a moment to understand what the girl was saying. Her voice was thick and slurred, as though her frozen lips and jaw didn't work very well. "Mother Hemlock?" Ollie whispered back, trying to neither stare at the wide, unblinking eyes nor flinch away from the black-tipped fingers. "Is she looking for you?"

"Always," whispered the girl. "Always. Sometimes she catches me. But I get away again. Now she won't find me. I'm hiding. I'm not afraid of the dark anymore. I can hide in the dark." She surveyed Ollie, and the blackened lips pressed down to nothing. "You're here too and you have to take care of yourself. Go away."

"You tried to warn me, didn't you?" said Ollie. "You said, *don't listen*. You showed me where to hide in the kitchen."

The girl didn't say anything, but Ollie had no intention of going away. She needed help, and she needed answers. She tried again, "Is your name Gretel?"

The girl shuddered, and slid away from Ollie. Her trembling mouth made an eerie contrast with her unblinking eyes. "Gretel? Was I? I can't remember now." Suddenly her calm, flat voice rose with panic. "I can't say anything else! He won't let me! How long have I been down here? An hour? Two? Not more. I can't remember now. But it doesn't matter. This is my hiding place. Go away!"

An hour? Ollie wondered. She opened her mouth to ask another question.

But she didn't. The footsteps had started up again. They were thumping somewhere on the stairs in the dark. Coming closer.

Ollie shut up and crouched low. Gretel, shivering, retreated deeper into the darkness. The footsteps got to the bottom of the stairs. They were the footsteps of a two-footed person. Not the bear, then. And they didn't sound like the clacking footsteps of Mother Hemlock. *Who was it?*

The footsteps paused, right at the base of the stairs.

Ollie peered cautiously around the lockers.

But there was no one there.

The footsteps continued, though. Foot by foot they went farther into the basement.

But what kind of ghost would be invisible here? Ollie wondered. She was on the bad side of the mirror. She should be able to see the ghosts. Ever since she'd come through the mirror, Ollie had seen all the ghosts. Mother Hemlock. The dead skier. This trembling girl.

Ollie thought she heard Gretel speaking softly to herself from the shadows. *"Don't listen,"* she was saying. *"Don't listen don't listen . . ."*

That was when Ollie heard the beeping.

She stiffened. That soft, steady beeping was *definitely* the sound of her mother's watch. But how could her mother's watch be here? The last time she'd seen it, her watch had been dangling between Seth's fingers. Was *Seth* here? All Ollie's muscles were tense, ready to run. But she kept still, listening hard.

The sound was coming from the open space right next to the oil lamp. Where the invisible person's footsteps had stopped.

"Hello?" Ollie whispered, her voice almost too low even for herself to hear. And, a little louder: "Hello? Mom?"

Silence. She waited, trembling.

Still nothing.

Then, in front of Ollie's startled eyes, Seth's Ouija board tumbled out of nowhere and hit the stone floor with a clatter.

———

When the watch started beeping loudly, Coco's first instinct was to clap her hand over it and muffle the noise so it wouldn't give her away. But as she did, she forgot about the Ouija board under her arm. It fell with a crash. Coco jumped back from the noise, breath coming panic-fast, wanting to run, not sure where to run *to*. The watch was still beeping. Why was it still beeping? Was it betraying her after all? Was this it?

The watch fell suddenly silent.

For a few seconds, there was no sound at all.

Then Coco heard footsteps. Soft, sneaking footsteps. They came out from behind a pile of dusty lockers. Coco strained her eyes into the dimness until they watered, but she couldn't see who was making the noise. The steps came nearer. Nearer. Coco started to back away, imagining cold, invisible ghostly hands reaching out.

But instead the footsteps paused. Right next to the Ouija board. And then, all by itself, the Ouija board turned right way up. It floated up and came down softly on the table, right next to the oil lamp.

Somehow, Coco didn't think it was Seth. "Is it the smiling man?" Coco whispered to the watch.

One beep. NO.

Silence fell again. A thick, expectant silence. There were no more footsteps. Coco, on sudden impulse, pulled the planchette out of her pocket, put it on the Ouija board, took a step back, and waited, heart beating fast.

Immediately the planchette started to move.

Don't trust it, Coco reminded herself. Last time the Ouija board had tricked them, tricked Ollie. This was probably another trick.

She was so busy reminding herself to watch out for tricks that she didn't notice the first couple of letters.

O R U, said the planchette, and stopped.

Huh? Coco had to think about that a second. She combed through her memory for the letters she'd missed. Oh. WHO R U.

Okay, Coco thought. Even if the invisible person was out to trick her, Coco might still learn something, if she talked to them. She'd just have to be on her guard for lies.

But her hand trembled when she put it down on the planchette. COCO, she spelled out. WHO U.

———

COCO, signed the planchette.

Ollie didn't know who she'd been expecting. It wasn't Coco.

But maybe it was fake. A lie? Vivid in Ollie's memory was the last time she'd used the Ouija board. *Don't trust anything it says,* she reminded herself.

But, oh, she wanted it to be Coco. Maybe she could test it, somehow? She put her shaking forefingers on the planchette. OLI, she signed. U HAV MOM WACH HOW.

The planchette didn't move for a second. Ollie's heart

183

beat with a mix of hope and terror. **PROVE U OLI 1ST**, said the planchette.

That *definitely* sounded like Coco. Despite herself, Ollie felt a surge of hope. She thought a second. **UR FAV CLR PRPL**, Ollie signed back. **FAV DESSERT PI**.

WUT KIND PI, returned the planchette. Ollie could almost feel her friend's suspicion.

APL, she said. **PROV U COCO**.

———

For the first time since Ollie disappeared through the mirror, Coco felt a sudden hope. How could the smiling man know all that? *Ollie, it's Ollie. She's talking to me.* **UR DAD CALL U OLLIEPOP, FAV CLR YLW**, she signed back. **FAV SNACK POPCRN**. Tears were stinging in her eyes. **GOT UR WACH BAK**.

The planchette didn't move for a second. Then, simply, it spelled out **TNX. HOW**.

LNG STRY. Coco felt that little flicker of pride again. She was glad she'd gotten the watch back. It was Ollie's most treasured possession. **U OK**, Coco signed.

YA BUT STUCK BHND MROR came the reply. **WHERE BRIAN**.

LOST HIM.

———

Ollie stared at the Ouija board. At first she'd just been happy that Coco was talking to her, that Coco had gotten Ollie's watch back. But now she was horrified. *Lost Brian?* How—lost?

HE OK, she signed.

The board—or Coco, on the other side—seemed to hesitate.

DUNNO, came the reply.

Ollie was so engrossed in watching the planchette whiz around the Ouija board that she totally failed to notice a new set of footsteps. Clomping down the stairs. They were nearly at the bottom before Ollie registered them, and then she threw herself away from the table, back into her hiding place behind the lockers.

She thought she heard a faint whimper of fear from Gretel, who was still hiding too, somewhere in the darkness.

Silence. Ollie peered out of her hiding place.

This time the person wasn't invisible. It was the ghost skier. Gabriel, maybe. He stood right in front of the staircase, peering left, then right, like he wasn't sure where to go. He was faceless in his ski mask. His hands pointed down at his sides, stiff with frostbite.

A garbled sound came from his ski mask. It sounded like a growl. It sounded terrifying. But Ollie wondered if it was just because his lips and jaw were frozen and he couldn't talk. Like Gretel but worse. He had tried to stop Mother Hemlock from taking her up to the closet. Ollie was almost sure that he had. Maybe he'd stopped her from coming down to the basement. Gotten ahead of her and blocked the door, somehow. Ollie hoped so. It was good to feel like she wasn't alone.

On the table, the planchette on the Ouija board was moving, but Ollie didn't dare take her eyes off the skier.

"Are you Gabriel?" Ollie asked, gathering her courage, stepping boldly out from her hiding place. "Gabriel Bouvier?"

An empty-eyed stare. Then a single, jerky nod.

"Can you talk?"

A shrug. An awkward head shake.

"Did you try to warn us? The person Coco saw, the first night, in the road. Was that you?"

Hesitation. Then a tiny nod.

"Did you try to help me? In the dining room?"

Another nod.

Ollie pointed down at the Ouija board. "Can you use that to talk?" she asked. "Can you move the letters?"

She thought he was doubtful, just by the way he stood still. "I have to get back through the mirror by dawn," Ollie told him. "Or else I'm stuck here. Please. If you can help me—just, please." Ollie didn't know what else to say. It wasn't like she could bribe him to help her or anything.

Or make him help her. But maybe asking was enough. He gave her a jerky nod. Ollie wished he wasn't wearing a ski mask. It was a bit like he didn't have a face at all. Hugely awkward in his giant, heavy orange ski boots, Gabriel went to the Ouija board. He turned his face to Ollie. *Now what?* he seemed to say.

Ollie took a place on the other side of the table. She thought she saw movement out of the corner of her eye; Gretel poked her head around her walls of boxes.

"Can I call you Gabe?" Ollie said to the ghost in the ski jacket. "My name's Ollie."

Another nod; she saw his hand tremble. Ollie wondered how long he'd been here. She wondered who the last person was to call him by name.

She decided she didn't want to find out. It would just make her scared. She said, "Wait a sec," put her hands on the planchette, and spelled, GABE BOUVIER GHOST HERE SAYS CN HLP HE GNA USE BORD 2 TLK.

A pause. Ollie could imagine Coco's expression going from surprised to nervous to frowning understanding. Then Coco's reply came back: K.

Gabe clumsily put one hand on the planchette. Ollie put her fingers on the planchette next to his frostbitten ones. Gabe's hand looked like a mummy's hand, but Ollie didn't flinch away. She was done with being scared of people—ghosts—who might look creepy but were trying to help. She was going to need all the help she could get, she thought, if she was ever to make it home again.

Slowly, with difficulty, Gabe began to slide the planchette.

———

OLI NEED OPN MROR AN GO THRU.

"Okay," whispered Coco, watching. Obviously they needed to open the mirror. Ollie was on the wrong side of it. **HOW OPN**, she signed.

FND BONES.

The Ouija board was like the worst text messenger ever, Coco thought in annoyance. She thought of Gretel, in the hallway of her nightmare. *I'm looking for my bones.*

GRTL BONES, she signed.

The planchette slid up to **YES**.

There were about a half dozen extremely important follow-up questions that Coco knew she had to ask. She picked one. **HOW CN GRTL BONES OPN MROR.**

BONES N REAL LODG, came the reply. **GHST N OTHR LODG WIT OLI. GHOST AND BONES CNNCTED IF R RFLCTD IN SAME MROR. WILL OPN DOR THRU MROR.**

———

Okay, Ollie thought. "I think I get it," she said aloud. "Gretel is on this side. Gretel's bones are somewhere on Coco's side. The ghost and her bones are connected. If Gretel stands in front of a mirror on my side, and her bones are reflected in the same mirror on Coco's side, then a door will open."

Gabe nodded slowly.

"But where are the bones?" said Ollie. "We know where Gretel is." She gestured back into the darkness where Gretel was hiding.

The planchette was moving again. Coco. Asking the same question. **WHR GRTL BONES**, she was asking.

———

DUNO, came the answer. **IN CLOSET I THNK. 2ND FLR.**

Coco ground her teeth. She'd had enough of those second-floor closets. But at the same time her heart was beating fast with hope. She could do that! She could go back up the stairs, use the watch to tell her which closet held Gretel's bones. The planchette was still moving. **BTR HURY**, it said. **SETH AN MTHR HMLCK TRY STOP U.**

"Tell me something I don't know," Coco muttered. She grabbed the planchette. There were more important questions. Quickly she spelled out **WHCH MROR, WHN MEET**, and **DUZ GABE NO WHR BRIAN**. The cold of the basement floor soaked into her socks as she whipped the planchette around the board.

Coco wished she could actually see Ollie and talk to

her properly. But she was desperately glad she'd grabbed the Ouija board. She didn't know what would have happened if she hadn't. She finished her questions, sat back. Waited for a reply.

BUNK RM MROR, said the Ouija board.

Okay, Coco thought. *But when?*

Coco waited for the rest. Nothing.

WHN, she signed impatiently.

The planchette wasn't moving.

"Ollie?" she whispered.

Just then the watch started to beep. Not slow and calm this time. No, loud and fast, like an alarm when you were late to school. Like a warning.

A blast of icy air whipped through the basement, and finally the planchette started to move again. But this time, Coco didn't think it was Ollie.

DO U KNO WHT HPNS TO THEVS, said the Ouija board.

Another cold gust whipped down through the stairwell, hard enough to instantly numb Coco's face. Up there, in the dark, she heard footsteps.

Then she heard Seth's voice. "Thieves are punished," he said.

Then the lamp went out.

14

A CLACKING FOOTSTEP landed on the dark staircase above Ollie. And a soft, hissing voice spoke out of the shadows. "Little mouse—where are you hiding? Where? Good little mice don't hide. *Where are you?*" Another footstep thumped on the staircase.

Ollie scrambled to her feet and back from the Ouija board just as she heard her mother's watch start beeping again. Loudly. Urgently. Invisibly. On the other side of the mirror.

Mother Hemlock was coming. Why hadn't she come before? Had Seth told her to wait? Why?

Clack. A foot landed on the steps in the darkness. *Clack.* Ollie's lips went stiff with fear; her skin felt tight and cold. Gabe's masked face showed no expression, but she saw his big shoulders go rigid under the rotten ski jacket.

Behind Ollie, Gretel whimpered, "You brought her here, you brought her here!"

Somewhere on the staircase, Ollie thought she heard the strange, grinding growl of the dead bear. Its stiff paws thudded on the stairs.

"No," Gretel was whispering to herself. "I'll be good, I'll be quiet, don't put me back with the others."

"Someone has been telling secrets," muttered Mother Hemlock from the staircase. *Clack, clack* went her footsteps. "Someone has been plotting. Someone is trying to run away. I know what to do with runaways."

Everything in the basement looked to Ollie as sharp as though it had been outlined in ink. The footsteps were coming nearer and nearer. Ollie turned to Gabe. "Is there another way out of the basement?"

Without a sound, he pointed away into the darkness.

"Okay," said Ollie. She had to force herself not to bolt, immediately, in the direction of Gabe's pointing finger. "Gretel, we have to go." If she needed Gretel to open the mirror, Ollie knew she couldn't lose her. The smiling man definitely wanted her and Gretel to be separated.

A gust of icy air swept through the basement, as though Mother Hemlock had breathed it out from the staircase.

Then the oil lamp went suddenly out. They were left

in the darkness, with Mother Hemlock's footsteps still descending. There was a soft wail from Gretel. "No! My light! Please, I'm tired of the dark."

The basement *was* dark. Coal-dark, moonless-night-camping dark. Darkness seemed to press on Ollie's eyelids, like it had a force all its own. Unable to see, Ollie froze; she didn't know which way to move. There were crates and boxes scattered all over the floor; she'd trip if she went three feet without light. Fumbling, Ollie pulled her book of matches out of her pocket and lit one.

Only to find Mother Hemlock right in front of her, inches away, smiling her wide, dead smile. "Can't hide," she said.

Ollie screamed. She hadn't screamed at the dead bear, or at Don Voland when he turned out to be the smiling man, but now she shrieked, pure fright and shock, and fell backward, hitting the icy stone floor hard. Her match went out, and in darkness, Ollie heard Mother Hemlock's whisper: "Not so disobedient now, are we? Well, up the stairs with you—"

Ollie smelled the old tombstone smell as Mother Hemlock reached down to grab Ollie by the ankle. But before she could, Ollie scrambled up and backward, and with shaking fingers, she seized and struck another match, all the while expecting to feel a cold, dead hand grabbing her.

But it didn't. Instead, Mother Hemlock shrieked, a horrible dry sound.

By the light of her match, Ollie saw a couple of things very quickly.

The dead bear was coming laboriously down the stairs. Its formaldehyde-filled legs didn't seem to work very well. Gabe had thrown an old sack of some kind over Mother Hemlock's head. She was groping around in a fury trying to get it off. Mother Hemlock, Ollie thought with a slightly hysterical part of her mind, looked way less scary with a bag over her head.

Ollie's match was about to start burning her fingers. Feverishly, she reached for the oil lamp, yanked off the glass cover, and relit the wick. The light wavered, steadied. She hoisted the lamp. Maybe carrying the light with her as she fled would give her away, but anything was better than facing that basement in the dead-screen dark.

Ollie turned toward the stairwell. The bear was almost at the bottom of the stairs. Its shoulders seemed to fill the whole space. She wasn't getting out past that, Ollie thought. She prayed that Gabe had been right about knowing another way out of the basement.

Gretel was crouched hiding in a corner. "Please," she was whispering. "Please, please, please go away. She's chasing you. Go away and she'll go too. But don't take my lamp. It's *mine*. It's the only thing I have. Don't take it."

Feeling horrible, Ollie lurched forward and grabbed the girl's wrist.

"If you don't come with me *right now*," Ollie said, "she'll get you. Come with me and I'll keep you safe. *I promise.* We'll have your lamp with us too."

Ollie was uncomfortably convinced that she was lying; she was pretty sure that Mother Hemlock wanted her more than Gretel right then, since Ollie still had a faint chance of escaping. Also she had no idea if she could keep Gretel safe. But she was desperate.

It wasn't nice. But it did work. Gretel stumbled to her feet and Ollie dragged her back toward Gabe.

Mother Hemlock managed to pull the cloth off her face. She was knocking over boxes to get at them.

Gretel's frozen eyes were newly horrified. "I told him no," she whispered to Gabe. "But you . . . you told him yes."

What did that mean, Ollie wondered. Gabe didn't move. Well, she could wonder later. "Come on," Ollie snapped. "We have to go."

Gabe was already gesturing them on—*hurry, hurry.* Holding Gretel's lamp high, Ollie followed him off into the basement shadows, gripping tight to Gretel's dry-dead ghost hand.

Behind them came Mother Hemlock's footsteps and the dry, heavy tread of the dead bear.

———

Coco was utterly frozen. Paralyzed by the darkness. It was like the world itself had blown out and left her in outer space. It was certainly cold enough for outer space. "Thieves stay in the basement," Seth's voice went on, snorting with laughter. "Until they have learned some manners."

Coco shrank away from that cold voice, quivering. Then she gathered her courage. "You're just a liar and a cheat!" she yelled into the darkness. "It's just tricks—all tricks!"

But no one answered. The basement had fallen silent once more. Then the oil lamp flickered back to life, as quickly as it had gone out, standing innocently on the table. Coco looked around. No Seth. She wasn't even sure she'd heard him at all. The watch had fallen silent.

But then Coco realized that in the darkness, two things had changed in the basement. The stairs were gone. Just—gone. There was only a blank brick wall where they had been.

The Ouija board was gone too.

He must have taken it, Coco thought. *Seth must have taken it when the lights were out.* She didn't know which to be more upset about, the loss of the board or the loss of the stairs.

She stared at the place where the stairs had been, blinked, stared again. It was like the stairs hadn't ever been there. But—maybe she wasn't remembering right? Maybe she'd gotten turned around in the dark? Maybe the stairs came out in a different place?

It was *possible*, she tried to encourage herself. Coco got lost easily. She picked up the oil lamp, lifted it high. She spun in a slow circle, staring at the walls.

Couldn't see any stairs.

The watch was silent. She looked down at its display. Still blank.

Coco's lips were numb with fear. There had to be a way out of the basement. Seth was just hiding it from her. Tricks. Like his voice in the stairwell, like the corridor that seemed to go on forever. He was trying to distract her until morning.

She had to find Gretel's bones before morning. She had to get back upstairs, to the second-floor corridor with the closets. She wished desperately for Ollie and Brian.

Okay, Coco told herself. *First things first. You have to get out of the basement.*

But Coco didn't know how to get out of the basement. She was trying not to panic again. It felt like the walls and the ceiling were going to start sliding closer and closer together any second now, until she was in a coffin, until her tiny light was extinguished and she would never get to see the sun ever again.

Coco shoved back against the panic. He was just

playing a game, the smiling man. Coco could play games too. She'd beaten him at chess, hadn't she? *You outsmarted that guy once,* Coco told herself grimly. *But now you're going to have to outsmart him again, and maybe again. Enough times to find the bones, and Brian, and get all three of us home.* The first step to outsmarting him was not to panic. He totally wanted her to panic.

No one, Coco knew, would really describe her as particularly smart. In class, when Coco got a good grade, teachers always gave her papers back with slightly puzzled compliments. It was part of being *tiny.* People would think you were eight. People would smile indulgently and ruffle her pink hair. But they didn't really think, *Hey, that's a clever girl.*

But Coco actually was smart. At least she thought she was. She was good at making plans. That was why she loved playing chess. Because you had to plan ahead. You had to try to think what the other person was thinking.

Now she had to try to think what the smiling man was thinking.

At chess tournaments, people when they saw her always went, *Oh, great, I'm playing the tiny girl. Easy win.*

Coco was pretty sure that was exactly what Seth had thought, seeing her. That was why he'd agreed to her chess challenge. Even why he'd separated her and Brian. Because he thought she couldn't win on her own.

But she could, Coco thought. She could.

There had to be a way out of the basement. Because all this was Seth's *game*. And where was the fun of playing a game when one side had no way to win?

Coco picked up the lamp, newly determined. First things first. The most obvious. Maybe the stairs were really there, but she just couldn't see them. She went to the wall. She started to walk along it, holding her lamp in one hand, running her fingers along the rough plastered brick with the other.

Nothing.

Now what? How much oil was left in her oil lamp? What would happen when it gave out? She stared around herself, trying to think.

Saw something on the floor.

Frowned. Peered closer. It was—snow? She reached out and touched it. It was icy cold on her fingers. Snow? Water? Tracks? How could there be snow in here? Had Seth tracked it in somehow, in the dark?

Then suddenly Coco remembered standing in front of a mirror in a long hallway. Remembered looking back the way they'd come. Remembered seeing footprints. Ghostly, snowy footprints. Her heart began to pound.

A ghost skier might make wet footprints. Gabe. Gabe had been in the basement, on Ollie's side of the mirror. Were these Gabe's footprints? Was he with Ollie now?

Had they found another way out of the basement? Coco strained to listen. Did she hear footsteps? Heavy footsteps, moving away from her? She thought she did. But she couldn't be sure.

"Should I follow?" Coco whispered to the watch.

Silence. Then two beeps. As though the watch were doubtful. Reluctant. But a YES.

"Okay," whispered Coco, trying to quiet her racing heart. Bending near to the floor, straining her eyes to find the tiny drips of snow and water, Coco began to wind her way through the maze of the basement.

15

OLLIE AND GABE and Gretel hurried through a labyrinth of boxes. Ollie's lantern lit things in flashes as she hurried. SUMMER CLOTHES. WINTER CLOTHES. GIRL SHOES. They couldn't run in a straight line, but had to stumble left and right, going around things.

The basement was huge. Neither Gretel nor Gabe could move very fast. Gabe was wearing ski boots. Gretel just stumbled a lot. They all made a lot of noise. Gabe's ski boots clomped on the stone floor, and Ollie's breathing sounded loud even to her own ears.

But then again, Ollie reasoned to herself grimly, she was carrying a giant lantern, so it wasn't like they were hard to spot.

She risked a glance back, but she couldn't see Mother Hemlock. Only hear her footsteps. *Clack. Clack.* The footsteps never seemed to hurry. But they never got any farther away either. Ollie thought of zombie movies, where the zombies wouldn't run, but wouldn't stop either. She fought off a shiver and tried to pull Gretel along faster.

"Oh, where are we going?" Gretel whispered. "Where? Where is it safe? You said we'd be safe."

"Out of here," Ollie whispered back. "I hope. And then my friend is going to help you find your bones. So you can go home. Isn't that what you needed? You said it in my dream. Your bones, so you could go home?"

Gretel let out a soft sigh. "Do you mean it?" she whispered. She stumbled again. For a second her clumsiness reminded Ollie of Coco, and Ollie felt a terrible surge of longing for her friend. "Do you promise? If you mean it, I'll let you have my lamp."

Ollie would have liked to promise. She wondered what the *real* story was, the history of the ghost girl, endlessly hiding, endlessly lost, and Mother Hemlock endlessly chasing. But she didn't know if *any* of them would make it out, let alone Gretel. And Ollie hated to lie *again*. So she just said, "I'll do my best. But first we have to hurry."

So Gretel did her best to hurry. Behind them, Mother Hemlock's footsteps were getting fainter. Maybe they were outrunning her! All they had to do was keep ahead of her, find a good hiding spot near the bunk room mirror, keep an eye on it, and hope Coco managed to find Gretel's bones.

Gabe halted suddenly. Ollie had to raise her lantern and squint after his pointing finger to be sure. But it was a door! Another door. Maybe a door out! It was narrow, set in a recess in the wall, and hard to spot. It had a tarnished handle and peeling paint. Ollie reached with her free hand, turned the knob, and opened the door.

Behind it was a skinny, dark staircase leading steeply up. Looking at those stairs, Ollie thought that she'd had enough of dark staircases to last her for the rest of her life.

Gretel was hanging back. "But," she said, "those stairs—"

Mother Hemlock's voice interrupted, whispering almost at their backs. "Where are you?" she breathed. "Where are you? I can smell deceit. I can *smell* bad children . . ."

With Mother Hemlock right behind them and the long staircase ahead, Ollie didn't hesitate. She pulled Gretel after her into the staircase and started to hurry up. Behind her, she heard Gabe close the lower door softly behind them and begin to climb heavily in their wake.

"Thanks for helping," Ollie whispered back to Gabe as she climbed. "It will be all right," she added to Gretel. "It will, it will . . ."

There was no sound from Gabe. Ollie had a tight grip on Gretel's wrist and was pulling her along. But the ghost girl was pulling back. "No," she was muttering to herself. "Don't listen, don't listen, don't listen . . . That's what I tried to tell you. But I'm so confused now. He wanted me to be confused. I don't remember why . . . Don't listen!"

As soon as they got off the stairs, Ollie decided, she was going to find a quiet place and try to understand what Gretel was talking about. But they had to get off the stairs first. Mother Hemlock was right behind them.

And they were almost off the stairs. Ollie could see a door in the wavering light of her oil lamp. "It's okay," she said. "It'll be okay, Gretel."

"No, it won't," said Gretel. Her voice shot up into a cry, like she'd suddenly understood. "It won't because—"

Ollie didn't hear the end of the sentence. She groped for the knob in the door at the top of the stairs, turned it.

And froze.

As the door swung open, Gretel let out a single, soft whimper of fear before she fell silent, standing rigid beside Ollie.

They were in a strange room. *No*, Ollie thought. *Not strange*. She'd seen it before.

In a nightmare.

It was the bunk room, but it wasn't. This room was not wide, but it was long. A thick hush lay over it. There were big black metal bars in the windows, and strong moonlight filtered in between them, throwing huge stripes of white light and shadow across the room. After the darkness of the basement, the moonlight dazzled her eyes.

Just like in Ollie's dream, the room was full of beds. In each bed was a girl asleep, with her eyes frozen shut.

Beside Ollie, Gretel whispered, her voice short and thin with fear, "Here? *Why would you bring me here?*"

Across from them and a little to their left, there was another door. This one had to lead out into the hall. Ollie licked dry lips. "We just have to get across the room," she said. "Come on."

Before they could move, someone sat up in the bed nearest them. It was a small girl. She looked a lot like Gretel. Same thin braided hair. Same frost-blackened nose.

Except that her eyes were packed with a thick layer of ice. Her eyes were frozen shut, not open.

But despite her closed eyes, she smiled, wide and empty. She turned her face toward them. And she spoke. "Gretel, you came back," she said, in a strange dry whisper. "Get in bed now, and she won't ever know you were gone."

Gretel started to tremble.

Another girl in another bed sat up. "Gretel, you brought a friend? No visiting after lights-out. Mother will be angry."

"So angry," said a third, also sitting up, and now there

were girls sitting up in all the beds, turning their ice-packed eyes, their wide smiles to Ollie and Gretel.

"It's okay," Ollie whispered. "Come on. I'll get you out of here."

She started to cross the room.

Gretel went along when Ollie pulled, but Ollie could feel her hand shaking.

"Gretel," a girl whispered. She had swung her legs out of bed; now she was standing, blocking their way. Another girl got up behind her. And another. They were blocking the way to the door. "Gretel, why did you run away?"

"Let us through!" snapped Ollie, and began to shove her way through the dead-eyed crowd. Gretel's hand was still shaking, and Ollie had started to shake herself. She felt like Mr. Wilson's deer must have felt, right before they were dragged down and mounted on the wall of Hemlock Lodge. She pushed on. "Come on, Gretel!" she snapped. "Don't stop."

Suddenly all the girls fell back with frightened shrieks. Ollie turned and felt a huge relief. Gabe had come into the dormitory and was plowing across the room toward them, head down, shoving his way through. Moonlight striped his blue ski jacket. The girls scrambled to get out of his way. He cleared a path to the door for Ollie and Gretel.

"Gabe," said Ollie. "Thank you so much." All the small ghost girls were cowering, back on their beds. Mother

Hemlock was nowhere in sight. It was going to be okay. Ollie reached for the door handle.

But Gabe was in front of her. Blocking her way.

"Gabe," said Ollie, "Gabe, move."

He didn't move. He looked down at her. This time, Ollie was close enough and the moonlight bright enough for Ollie to see his eyes above the ski mask.

He had the saddest eyes Ollie had ever seen.

He crossed his arms. He didn't move. He was blocking the door.

"No!" cried Gretel. "No, please let us out!" She tried to grab the doorknob. But Gabe just shook his head. He made the most terrible effort to speak that Ollie had ever heard. But nothing came out that she could understand.

Instead a voice spoke from behind her. Seth's voice.

Slowly, Ollie turned around.

"He lied, you know," said Seth. "Ghosts do not like to lie. But they can. If they are properly motivated."

He looked like plain Mr. Voland. He was wearing his green shirt, his jeans. Even in the moonlight, she could see the freckles over his nose. But his eyes had a red gleam, like reflected firelight. Maybe it was just the guttering lamp in Ollie's hand, shining in his eyes.

But she didn't think so.

Then Ollie blinked and Mr. Voland was gone; instead she saw Seth as she'd seen him in the corn maze, with bone-colored hair and cold blue eyes. Ollie wondered, trembling, if he had a real face at all or if he just picked one as it suited him.

"Gabe's been here a long time," said Seth. "It was easy enough to promise him freedom for a few lies, a little misdirection. And you made it so easy, when Coco stole my Ouija board."

Beside Ollie, Gretel moaned.

"She wanted to warn you," said Seth, with a jerk of his chin. "She might have tried, I believe. But the poor brave thing's been here so long, she hardly knows what's real anymore." His smile was broad and hungry. Triumphant. He knew he'd won.

Don't listen, Ollie thought in horror. *Don't listen to the dead voices.* That was what Gretel had said. But Ollie had listened. She'd listened twice. And she'd been caught twice.

A horrible gargling sound came from Gabe's throat. It took Ollie a second before she understood.

Sorry. He was trying to say sorry.

"Checkmate," said Seth. "Not much of an adversary, are you, without your watch helping you?"

Ollie licked her lips, tried to think of something to say. Couldn't think of anything. She had to get out of this room.

"Farewell," said Seth, and disappeared.

The next second, Mother Hemlock burst into the

bunk room. She was smiling. Ollie whipped around and tried once more, in desperation, to force a way past Gabe. But he blocked her, although he trembled as he did. *"Have to,"* he whispered. "Have to." His eyes over the ski mask were dark and desperate.

"Girls," said Mother Hemlock to the crowd of watching ghosts. Her thin, scratching voice rang with triumph. "Your little classmates have come back. But it seems they want to leave us! So soon! Do we want them to leave, girls?"

"No," whispered the girls, like a chorus of snakes.

Ollie flung Gretel's oil lamp at Mother Hemlock. It was the only thing she could think of. But it didn't work. The lamp rolled past and away under a bed. The glass broke; the fire went out. And then the room was lit only by moonlight. Gretel cried out, "No! My light!" and knelt weeping by the broken glass.

Ollie looked left and right. There was nowhere to run. They were hemmed in by beds, by Gabe, by the little ghost girls with their eyes frozen shut but somehow still watching.

"Time for bed," said Mother Hemlock, coming closer. "Time for you to sleep like good little girls." Her voice was gentle now. "I won't even put you in the closet. Just lie down."

"No!" Gretel screamed, looking up. "No, I don't want to."

Ollie charged straight at Mother Hemlock, hoping to get past her, maybe go down the basement stairs again. Something. But a large cold hand grabbed her arm as she ran past.

"Troublesome girl!" said Mother Hemlock. "Go to sleep."

To her horror, Ollie felt her eyelids growing heavy. She turned to look at Gretel. Gretel stared back at her, desperation in her face. Frost was stealing up over her eyes, sealing them shut. Ollie screamed when she felt the frost creeping up over her own face.

"Go to sleep," said Mother Hemlock. "Soon you'll be ours forever, and I'll have done all he wanted. He'll give me this place to be mine forever. Just sleep till dawn."

No, Ollie screamed. *No, I won't. You can't make me.*

But she realized she was only screaming in her head. No sound came out. Her eyelids were heavy as marbles. She felt herself sinking to the floor. *Dad*, she thought, right before a thick sleep claimed her, *I'm sorry. I hope Coco and Brian are okay. I tried. I really tried.*

Then she thought, *If I was stuck here, like Gabe, maybe I would have done it too.*

And finally she thought, *Mom?*

Then nothing.

16

COCO *THOUGHT SHE* saw a door in the basement wall. Just caught a tiny glimpse of a narrow door with a tarnished handle. Her triumph didn't last long. Just as she reached for it, the oil lamp went out and the glass part shattered, sending shards everywhere, cutting her fingers. Coco gasped and nearly dropped the lamp.

It was completely dark now, and her lamp had broken out of nowhere. What had happened? Coco froze. Listening, since she couldn't see. But this time she heard nothing. There was no cold breeze, no strange voice, no footsteps. Why had the lamp broken? Coco wished she'd grabbed matches from the lobby desk earlier, like she'd seen Ollie do, so she could relight it.

Well, at least she'd found the door before her light went out. She was just going to have to climb in the dark. Coco took a tighter grip on her broken oil lamp, unwilling to leave even the possibility of light behind. Groping ahead, she opened the basement door and started stumbling her way up the stairs.

There was no light. None at all; she had to climb by touch, feeling the steps with her toes, straining her ears. Her imagination turned every creak of the staircase into another person's footsteps and every hiss of her clothes into ghostly, whispering voices. Coco wiped her palms on her flannel pants and kept going, gritting her teeth. It was the worst possible situation for a clumsy person. The staircase was very narrow, and the steps seemed to be all different heights. She kept catching her feet painfully on taller-than-expected steps and almost falling.

It didn't help that her toes and fingertips were numb. The lodge was freezing.

She was so busy concentrating on not stubbing her toes that the door at the top took her by surprise. In fact, she ran into it face-first with a bang and nearly knocked herself out.

She almost fell backward down the stairs, caught herself, and then just stood there in the dark for a second, panting. She tasted blood, realized that she'd split her lip on the door. She thought a couple of very bad words. Then, scowling ferociously, she put her hand on the doorknob and came stumbling out.

She stopped short in surprise. She'd come through the door into her and Ollie's room.

"Okay," she muttered. "That's weird." Then the sound of her own voice made her jumpy, so she didn't say anything else. She tried the light switch. Didn't work. Figured.

But Coco could still see just fine. The room was full of moonlight. After the inky darkness on the stairwell, the moonlight was bright enough to make her blink. The storm must be over. Stepping cautiously, she crossed the room and threw wide the half-closed curtains. Beyond the window was the huge sweep of mountain and trees and ski lift, and the huge heaps of snow, still and sparkling. Coco took a deep breath. It was good to see the sky.

Then she noticed that, even with the curtains wide open, the moonlight fell in stripes across the room, as though there were bars across the window. But there weren't.

Coco spun, looking around the room. The moonlight was bright, but tricky; she had to squint into the corners, looking for anything out of place. Like a shadow with nothing there to cast it.

But everything seemed normal. Her and Ollie's stuff was on the floor, Ollie's spread out and messy, the way they'd left it that morning. The sight hurt. Coco clenched her fists and kept looking.

Then movement caught her eye. Coco's head jerked up. Something was moving in the big mirror over the dresser. Coco went closer. "Ollie," she whispered. Ollie was in the mirror. She was standing, facing gray-faced Mother Hemlock. Behind her stood the guy in the ski mask. Gabe. He was blocking the door. Keeping Ollie in the room.

He wasn't helping Ollie, Coco thought in rising horror. He was helping Mother Hemlock, helping Seth.

He'd betrayed them.

Coco watched as Ollie tried to dart past Mother Hemlock. But even as she tried, Coco saw the ghost woman reach out and touch her friend, lightly, on the face.

Ollie tried to keep running. But she couldn't. Her eyes got heavy; she stumbled and half fell, like she was falling asleep on her feet. Shaking, Coco saw a rime of frost creeping up Ollie's face, sealing her eyes shut.

Coco remembered the frostbitten ghost girl at the top of the stairs. Knew what would happen to Ollie if Coco couldn't get her out.

Ollie slumped to the floor, asleep. At least Coco hoped Ollie was asleep, and nothing worse. Coco had both her palms pressed to the glass in the mirror. "Ollie!" she screamed. "Ollie!"

But her friend didn't twitch. Mother Hemlock had picked her up. She heaved Ollie into one of the rows of narrow beds. The moonlight had a strange blurring effect, flattening Ollie's face, draining out Ollie's personality, so that Coco wouldn't have known which one was her friend at all, except for her curling hair.

"Ollie," Coco whispered. Ollie didn't look, though. She didn't even twitch. No one looked, except for the skier. Gabe. He looked sadly up and straight out at her.

The watch beeped softly. Bleakly.

"They got her, didn't they?" said Coco. "Seth and Mother Hemlock. Just like that."

Two beeps. Slow and sad. YES.

Coco felt strangely calm. It was as though she'd burned through all her fear, of the dark, of everything, and now she was calm. Determined. No Ollie, no Brian. But she was still free. Gretel—the ghost girl Coco recognized from the stairs, from her nightmare—was being bundled into a bed next to Ollie. If only Coco could race out into the corridor, find the bones, and then come back and . . .

But then Coco thought, *Hang on. Bones?* Gabe had told them about the bones. Gabe had betrayed Ollie.

Why was she trusting anything Gabe said? Maybe she didn't need *bones* at all. Maybe—

Torn, Coco looked back into the mirror and recoiled.

Right on the other side of the glass was Mother Hemlock. Watching Coco.

She smiled at Coco. Tapped the glass of the mirror. Her lips moved, and though Coco couldn't hear her, she saw what Mother Hemlock was saying.

Soon.

Coco wanted to say something brave and clever. But she couldn't really think of anything. She was cold and tired and alone and most desperately scared.

But even as she stared into Mother Hemlock's dead face, she was still thinking. Seth hadn't wanted her to have Ollie's watch. He hadn't wanted her to have the Ouija board either. He'd come into the basement and taken the board back. But why? If he wanted Gabe to lie to her, tell her the wrong things, then why take the board away again?

Coco thought of Gretel's bones. They'd heard a lot about Gretel's bones. From dreams, from Gabe.

But she couldn't trust Gabe.

Maybe Seth, Coco thought, wanted her to be chasing Gretel's bones until dawn.

But if not the bones, then what?

Coco thought of the world behind the mist. To get back from there, they'd needed something that existed on both sides. They'd used a book called *Small Spaces*. That was why having Gretel and her bones to open the mirror had seemed reasonable to Coco. Because *Gretel* was something—someone—who existed on both sides.

But what if it didn't have to be Gretel and her bones? What if it could be . . .

That was when Coco noticed it.

Just peeking out from under Ollie's bed. The oil lamp. The oil lamp that had broken in her hand down in the basement. It had fallen. It lay on its side, just showing, halfway under Ollie's bed. It was broken too.

It was on both sides of the mirror, Coco realized. Like the Ouija board.

There is a way to win, Seth had said.

Coco tried to remember everything she'd seen when Ollie went through the mirror the first time.

Two things reflected in both sides of the mirror.

One of them was the fire.

Coco thought. And she thought. She glanced down at the watch. Glanced back at sleeping Ollie.

But before she could make up her mind, Seth appeared in the mirror beside Mother Hemlock.

"Well," he said composedly.

Coco actually heard his voice. Not from the mirror. Coco spun around. He was standing in the middle of her room, her side of the mirror, hands in his pockets. "Well, that's that," he said. "She's not coming back through now, even if you open the way. She'll sleep until dawn. It didn't go too well for you tonight, did it? Despite the thing on your wrist. Although it has been delightful watching you try."

Coco didn't say anything.

Seth raised an eyebrow at the row of beds in the mirror, at Ollie in one of them. "Olivia is really too trusting. First Mr. Voland, then that boy in the ski boots. Really. A little mistrust, and she wouldn't be in this mess at all."

"Where's Brian?" asked Coco.

Seth grinned at her. "Lost," he said. "You'd be surprised where the doors lead in this lodge tonight. *He* certainly has been surprised. I made sure he got lost and stayed lost. I doubt you'll find him before dawn. If you like," he added, with a kindly air that made Coco feel faintly sick, "you can give up now. Go through this minute, go to sleep on the bed next to your friend, and you won't even notice the dark."

"Thanks, but no thanks," said Coco. "It's not dawn yet."

"No," he said. "But soon."

Coco said, "Are you going to shove me through the mirror right now?"

"Where would the fun be in that?" He had dimples when he smiled. Somehow the fact that he was enjoying himself made it all a lot worse.

"Fine," said Coco. "Then I'm leaving. I'm going to figure out how to save Ollie." She turned for the door.

Realized that there were now three doors leading out of the room. She stopped and looked back.

Seth laughed. "Do as you like. You can play my games until dawn, if you wish. But then—through the mirror."

And then he was gone. Not like disappearing in a puff of smoke or anything. No, just, one second he was there, and Coco blinked and then he wasn't.

17

WELL, THIS IS DUMB was Coco's first thought. It wasn't like she was stuck in the bunk room. She had the watch. All she had to do was ask it to beep when she stood in front of the correct door. She could get away from the horrible sight of Ollie asleep, eyes frozen shut.

But—Coco had an idea. It was a very risky idea. But it was the only one she could think of. She just needed the answers to a couple of questions first. She thought she knew how to get them. Maybe, she thought, Seth had made a mistake when he had the basement stairs lead up to this room. Probably he'd wanted her to see that mirror, to see what had happened to Ollie, so Coco would get scared.

Coco was scared. But she had an idea.

She dove for her stuff, still scattered on the bunk room floor. She scrabbled among her belongings, came up with a marker and paper. "I'm going to ask a couple of questions.

After each question, I'm going to read out the alphabet," she told the watch. "Stop me at the right letters, to spell out an answer."

The watch beeped twice.

Coco asked, talking as softly as she could, barely moving her lips, in case Seth was listening, "How do I wake up Ollie?"

She started reading the alphabet. All around, the lodge was completely, utterly still. Coco didn't like the stillness. It felt like there were eyes in the shadows. Watching. Waiting.

CAL HER BY NAME, said the watch. BUT U MUST BE ON HR SID MROR.

That was what Coco had been afraid of. She took a shaky breath.

Next question.

"Are you a part of Ollie?"

She started reading the alphabet again.

ALWAYS, said the watch.

"Okay," said Coco. "Then I know what I'm going to do."

18

COCO STARTED TO CRY. It wasn't hard. She'd had a lot of tears pent up inside her. She fell to her knees and sobbed, staring at Seth's stupid three exits, the three doors that—maybe—led from the bunk room. "I can't," she whispered. "I can't. Please. Please stop. I don't want to play anymore."

Next second, the left-hand door to the room flew open and Brian came stumbling in, wild-eyed. He saw Coco.

"Coco!" he cried. "I ran down the hallway. I ran and I ran and finally got to a door, but it just opened into the kitchens, or closets, or the Wilsons' living room . . ." He was shaking, wild-eyed. "And I couldn't find you."

Coco hugged him tightly. *It's working,* she thought, heart hammering. The smiling man would only let Brian find her if he thought she was beaten. He liked to gloat; he'd want to gloat in front of them both.

Maybe he was right, and they were beaten. After all, Coco only had the one impossible idea. But at least she and Brian could try it together. She was so glad to see her friend. "It's not over yet," she said as softly as she could. But she let the tears pour from her eyes.

"Are you okay?" Brian asked in alarm, seeing her sob.

Coco didn't answer; she had her eyes on the shadows of the moonlit bunk room. One of the shadows, she noticed, was human-shaped. She raised her eyes to the mirror and Gabe was standing there just behind Mother Hemlock. Both ghosts were watching them. Mother Hemlock looked gleeful. Expectant. Gabe just looked sad.

Brian looked up, following Coco's gaze. He recoiled from their dead, stiff faces.

Inside, Coco was tense as a spring. But on the outside, she let herself keep on crying. "I'm sorry, Brian," she sobbed. "I'm so sorry. I didn't find Gretel's bones. I'm so sorry."

Brian just stared at her, bewildered. "No," he said. "What bones? It's okay, it's not dawn yet. We're not beaten, we're not."

In chess, there was a move called a feint. The opposing player makes an aggressive move on one part of the board, to draw your attention. Like Coco had done with her queen when she played chess with the smiling man.

223

The thing about a feint is it's just a trick. A ploy. A way to mask a much more subtle, simple, and straightforward attack somewhere else.

So Coco let herself cry. She was pretty sure it was what Seth was expecting her to do. Just a little pink-haired girl crying.

Ollie's watch felt cold under her fingers.

Coco kept crying. But, quickly, she pulled off Ollie's watch, handed it to Brian. "Don't follow me," she whispered, between sobs. "That lamp"—she jerked her chin at the oil lamp—"is going to light in a second, I hope. Make sure it doesn't go out."

Brian stared at her tearstained face. She gave him a fierce stare. He'd trusted her during the chess game. This wasn't chess.

Or maybe it kind of was.

Brian, without saying a word, just took the watch and nodded once.

Coco turned back to Gabe. Quickly and quietly, she said, "If you were ever a person, ever even a little bit of a good person, answer me: Ollie has matches, doesn't she?"

Gabe stared at her. He still looked guilty. Then he nodded.

"Where?" Coco demanded.

"Front pocket," he whispered.

They didn't have time for more. Seth swept into the room. "Change your mind?" he asked airily. Coco still had tears on her face. It was no effort at all to keep on sobbing.

"I give up," she whispered. "We give up. I'm tired of being scared. I don't want to be scared until dawn. Can I—can I go through now? I want it to be over. Please. I just want it to be over." Coco buried her face in her hands and cried shrill, desperate, beaten tears.

"Surprising," said Seth. "Despite your appearance, I thought you'd have more backbone."

Coco just let her eyes fill again. "Please," she said. "Please, enough."

Brian was staring at Coco, and the horror in his voice wasn't faked when he said, "Coco, what are you doing?"

"I just don't want to be scared anymore," said Coco. "If we go through the mirror, we'll just sleep on a bed, just like the other ghost children. They're not scared. Like Ollie." She waved at the mirror, saw Brian catch sight of Ollie and bite his lip so hard it bled. "We won't be scared when we're sleeping."

"I won't!" snapped Brian. "I won't go through the mirror! You can't make me!"

Seth said, "I fear that you will find that I can. After all, that was the price of losing."

"Don't be scared," said Coco. "Soon we won't be

scared at all." She gave Brian a long look. She couldn't say *trust me*, but she tried to let her eyes say it for her.

Seth said a single word that made the air smell like rotten eggs, and the mirror rippled once.

It was open.

Coco, heart beating rabbit-fast, crossed the room, put both her hands on the mirror, stepped forward, and found herself in a moonlit mirror world.

Behind her, she heard Seth say, "Your turn," to Brian.

But Coco wasn't even paying attention to Seth anymore. Because she had her eye on three things. One was Ollie herself, lying asleep in the bed directly across from her.

Another was the oil lamp, lying abandoned.

The third was Mother Hemlock, standing there waiting for her. Coco seized the blanket off Ollie's bed and flung it over Mother Hemlock's head, winning herself a few seconds. "Ollie!" she screamed. *"Olivia Adler, you have to wake up!"*

The sound of her friend's voice answering made her weak with relief.

"Coco?" Ollie's voice filled with horror. "I can't see you. You—no—you can't be here?"

Coco didn't answer. She had dived for the oil lamp under Ollie's bed. There was a little oil in the chamber. "Ollie, your matches, *right now*," Coco snapped.

Ollie, without another word, dug into her pocket, grabbed a matchbook, and, with trembling hands, lit one. Her eyes were still frozen shut; she was working by touch. Coco brought her the lamp, and the wick kindled just as Mother Hemlock's hand descended.

Coco whipped around, holding the lamp, just as she saw fire bloom in the mirror on the other side. The lamps were connected. She had been right.

And now there was fire on both sides of the mirror.

Mother Hemlock recoiled from the flames. But Coco's blood went cold, because she saw Seth reaching for the lamp, obviously meaning to put it out on the other side. His mouth twisted; he'd seen what Coco was trying to do.

Mother Hemlock was coming for her; Coco shoved the burning lamp in her face; she cringed away.

"Brian!" she shouted, praying that Brian could hear. "Keep the fire going!"

Brian was a very practical person. But in this case, maybe desperation or the long, terrible night made him too quick to decide what to do. Rather than risk Seth smothering the lamp, he set the curtains on fire.

The curtains on the ghost side of the mirror went up too, sending living, golden light across rows and rows of dead faces. Coco, figuring that she couldn't make things worse, threw down her own lamp so that it spilled oil over the floor and set fire to it.

Well, she thought, giddy with rage, terror, alarm, and exhaustion, *I really hate this lodge. And now we have fires on both sides of the mirror.*

"Come on," she said to Ollie. "Time to go."

Ollie looked confused. Meltwater was running like tears down her face. "Where is Gretel?" she said. "What about the bones?"

"No time to explain!" yelled Coco. Fire was already roaring all around them. She grabbed her friend's hand and ran full-speed at the mirror.

Either I'm right, Coco thought, *or we're trapped forever in a burning building.*

They slammed into the glass.

And through it. Brian was already red-eyed from the smoke. *"How?"*

"Tell you in a minute," said Coco. "The lodge is on fire."

Seth was still there. He stared at her with an expression Coco could only describe as *fascinated horror.*

Coco couldn't resist. She grinned at him and she hoped her smile was as scary as his had been.

"Checkmate," she said, and pointed at Brian, who had put Ollie's watch on his wrist. Seth's lips tightened, seeing it. He looked from the watch to Ollie herself, who was still leaning on Coco, the ice thawing from her eyes. Coco saw him understand what she'd done.

The room was full of smoke. But she didn't care.

From the hallway came the reassuring wail of a fire alarm. Through the burning curtains, outside the window, she saw a pearl-pink dawn and a world lying under a perfect blanket of snow. "I tricked you in the chess game," she said to Seth. "And you tried to trick me. You tried to distract me with those stupid bones. We were supposed to spend the whole night chasing around the lodge for them. When the answer was just Ollie, and her watch. Or maybe even the Ouija board would have worked, if we'd known. Something that exists on both sides of the mirror opens a doorway through it. And I guess the fire helps too."

Seth looked torn between anger and admiration. Coco's two friends were on either side of her. "We won," said Ollie strongly. Water was running like rain down her face and her eyes were open and bright now. "Coco won. Go away."

"Guys," said Brian practically. "Forget him. He's just a jerk, and he tried to come here and mess with us, but he lost. Does anyone know where there is a fire extinguisher?"

Coco had expected Seth to look furious. But his face was completely expressionless. That scared her worse, somehow.

Then he bowed suddenly, an old-fashioned gesture that looked completely natural. His eyes were suddenly bright, and he smiled his wild-wolf smile at them.

"Until next time," he said, and then the smoke billowed up and he disappeared.

The three of them were already choking on smoke. They ran for the door of the room. But not before Coco looked back at the mirror and saw the ghosts on the other side dissolving into smoke and fire with looks of profound relief on their faces.

Thank you, mouthed Gretel. And vanished into the light.

19

OLLIE, BRIAN, AND COCO found the fire extinguisher just as Mr. Adler came thundering up the stairs with Coco's mom and the Wilsons on his heels. Mr. Adler saw the smoke, saw the fire extinguisher, grabbed it out of Brian's hands, and used it on the burning floor, the burning curtains. Mr. Wilson had another fire extinguisher, and after a few tense seconds, the overhead sprinklers came on, drenching everyone.

A small silence fell when the fire was out.

Ollie, Brian, and Coco were all red-eyed and coughing from lack of sleep and from the smoke. They stood there. None of them knew what to say.

"What happened?" asked Ollie's dad.

"We heard the fire alarm," said Ollie glibly. She was still coughing. "And ran upstairs. You guys slept so hard.

But it was okay; Brian's a Boy Scout and he grabbed the fire extinguisher. It's okay now. It's okay." Ollie was babbling. Then she burst into tears, ran over, and hugged her dad. Her dad hugged her back, looking a little puzzled.

"Coco," said her mom. "What happened to your lip?"

Coco ran her tongue over it, where she'd split her lip on the door. "Oh," she said, and waved an arm. "I tripped. Um, so did Brian." Brian had a split lip too.

Her mom raised an eyebrow.

"Going to the bathroom," Coco improvised. "It was—uh, slippery."

Brian nodded jerkily.

"Oh," said her mom practically. "Well, we'll have to disinfect it, then." Her mom hugged her, and hugged Brian for good measure.

Outside, Coco could see the sun rising over Mount Hemlock. It was really over. They had won.

She had won.

Ollie stepped back from her dad, wiping her eyes. "I don't know about you guys," said Ollie, "but I want to go home today. Sorry. It's just—it was a weird night. I want to go home." She nodded apologetically at the Wilsons. But they barely heard her. They were going through the bunk room, annoyed at the smoke damage and the broken mirror.

"Okay," said Mr. Adler, looking at Ollie with concern. She was white as a sheet, her face wet with tears and meltwater. "Is that what you want, Ollie-pop?"

Ollie nodded.

"Then let's get packing," said her dad.

Ollie, Brian, and Coco hurried to get their stuff.

They went back to the Egg that same day, leaving Hemlock Lodge without a backward glance as soon as they had dug out Susie and plow trucks had cleared the road. Neither Mr. Adler nor Coco's mom objected at all to their leaving.

"I had the weirdest dreams," said Mr. Adler to Ollie. "You were lost, and I couldn't find you." He shook his head. "It was terrible. Must have been the cold. Such a cold night last night, huh?"

"Yeah, it was," said Ollie, shuddering. She got into the car and closed her eyes with relief. Coco and Brian were right behind her. As they peeled out of the lodge parking lot, Ollie asked, "Can we make waffles at home?"

"Definitely," said her dad.

Ollie, Brian, and Coco all fell asleep in the car on the way back to the Egg. They barely woke up enough to shovel down waffles before they crawled onto beds and couches and went to sleep again.

"Poor kids," Coco heard her mom say as she drifted

off to sleep again. "That weird day in the lodge must really have stressed them out."

You have no idea, Mom, Coco thought.

———

They finally woke up enough to eat dinner properly, and afterward they sat on beanbags on the floor of Ollie's room, eating apple pie.

"But," said Ollie a little plaintively, "I still don't get it. The bones were . . ."

"Maybe not a lie, exactly," said Coco. "But a distraction. A feint. Like in chess. It just—I felt like it kept being thrown in our faces. Dreams about Gretel's bones, and Gabe telling us about Gretel's bones. But Gabe was working for the smiling man. How trustworthy could he be? And then I thought about the world behind the mist. Remember? Seth used scarecrows, visible in both worlds, to hold the door open between them. But, Ollie, that time, you got us home because the book *Small Spaces* existed in both worlds. So I was like, well duh, more than one thing can open a door between worlds, or hold one open. Why did it have to be Gretel and her bones? Why couldn't it be Ollie and her watch? I wasn't sure about the fire, but I figured lighting the lamps couldn't hurt since there was a fire in both sides of the mirror when you went through the first time, Ollie."

"Wow," said Brian. "BK, you were brilliant."

"BK?" asked Coco.

"You're the Black Knight," said Brian solemnly, and Coco grinned.

"I guess I am," she said.

"I hope they're all okay now," said Ollie, low-voiced. "Gabe and Gretel and the rest. I hope the fire set them free."

"I think it did," said Coco.

"That's good, then," said Ollie.

None of them said anything for a second. Then Brian asked, "You guys want to ski tomorrow? We could just go up to the Punch Bowl."

The Punch Bowl was their local mountain. It was small and friendly.

"That sounds fun," said Coco. After the night before, no ski mountain would ever scare her again. "Just don't leave me behind."

"You didn't leave us behind," said Ollie seriously. "Why would we ever do that to you?"

Brian nodded. Coco felt herself smiling.

But that night, just as they were falling asleep, Coco heard Ollie's voice from the bed. Coco was on an air mattress next to her. "Hm?" she asked.

"I said," Ollie repeated, "do you think he's really coming back? The smiling man?"

"I don't know," said Coco. She had to be honest. "Maybe—probably. But next time we'll be ready."

"Yup," said Ollie. "We'll be ready."

Ollie pulled out her watch. Coco had given it back to her in Hemlock Lodge. The word LOVE had returned to the watch face. Ollie held it to her cheek a moment.

"Thanks, Mom," she said softly. "I love you."

"Thanks a lot," Coco added from the floor.

Then Ollie tucked the watch under her pillow, and they all fell asleep to the quiet of a windless winter night, and Mr. Adler and Coco's mom playing music very softly downstairs.

Turn the page
for a sample of Katherine Arden's . . .

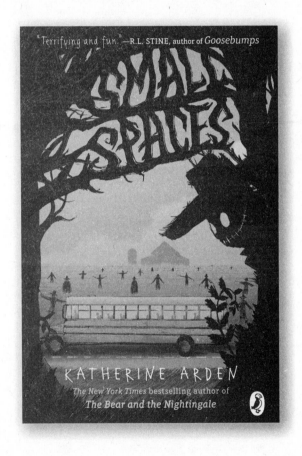

1

OCTOBER IN EAST EVANSBURG, and the last warm sun of the year slanted red through the sugar maples. Olivia Adler sat nearest the big window in Mr. Easton's math class, trying, catlike, to fit her entire body into a patch of light. She wished she were on the other side of the glass. You don't waste October sunshine. Soon the old autumn sun would bed down in cloud blankets, and there would be weeks of gray rain before it finally decided to snow. But Mr. Easton was teaching fractions and had no sympathy for Olivia's fidgets.

"Now," he said from the front of the room. His chalk squeaked on the board. Mike Campbell flinched. Mike Campbell got the shivers from squeaking blackboards and, for some reason, from people licking paper napkins. The sixth grade licked napkins around him as much as possible.

"Can anyone tell me how to convert three-sixteenths to a decimal?" asked Mr. Easton. He scanned the room for a victim. "Coco?"

"Um," said Coco Zintner, hastily shutting a sparkling pink notebook. "Ah," she added wisely, squinting at the board.

Point one eight seven five, thought Olivia idly, but she did not raise her hand to rescue Coco. She made a line of purple ink on her scratch paper, turned it into a flower, then a palm tree. Her attention wandered back to the window. *What if a vampire army came through the gates right now? Or no, it's sunny. Werewolves? Or what if the Brewsters' Halloween skeleton decided to unhook himself from the third-floor window and lurch out the door?*

Ollie liked this idea. She had a mental image of Officer Perkins, who got cats out of trees and filed police reports about pies stolen off windowsills, approaching a wandering skeleton. *I'm sorry, Mr. Bones, you're going to have to put your skin on—*

A large foot landed by her desk. Ollie jumped. Coco had either conquered or been conquered by three-sixteenths, and now Mr. Easton was passing out math quizzes. The whole class groaned.

"Were you paying attention, Ollie?" asked Mr. Easton, putting her paper on her desk.

"Yep," said Ollie, and added, a little at random, "point

one eight seven five." Mr. Bones had failed to appear. Lazy skeleton. He could have gotten them out of their math quiz.

Mr. Easton looked unconvinced but moved on.

Ollie eyed her quiz. *Please convert 9/8 to a decimal. Right.* Ollie didn't use a calculator or scratch paper. The idea of using either had always puzzled her, as though someone had suggested she needed a spyglass to read a book. She scribbled answers as fast as her pencil could write, put her quiz on Mr. Easton's desk, and waited, half out of her seat, for the bell to ring.

Before the ringing had died away, Ollie seized her bag, inserted a crumpled heap of would-be homework, stowed a novel, and bolted for the door.

She had almost made it out when a voice behind her said, "Ollie."

Ollie stopped; Lily Mayhew and Jenna Gehrmann nearly tripped over her. Then the whole class was going around her like she was a rock in a river. Ollie trudged back to Mr. Easton's desk.

Why me, she wondered irritably. Phil Greenblatt had spent the last hour picking his nose and sticking boogers onto the seat in front of him. Lily had hacked her big sister's phone and screenshotted some texts Annabelle sent her boyfriend. The sixth grade had been giggling over them all day. And Mr. Easton wanted to talk to *her*?

Ollie stopped in front of the teacher's desk. "Yes? I turned in my quiz and everything so—"

Mr. Easton had a wide mouth and a large nose that drooped over his upper lip. A neatly trimmed mustache took up the tiny bit of space remaining. Usually he looked like a friendly walrus. Now he looked impatient. "Your quiz is letter-perfect, as you know, Ollie," he said. "No complaints on that score."

Ollie knew that. She waited.

"You should be doing eighth-grade math," Mr. Easton said. "At least."

"No," said Ollie.

Mr. Easton looked sympathetic now, as though he knew why she didn't want to do eighth-grade math. He probably did. Ollie had him for homeroom and life sciences, as well as math.

Ollie did not mind impatient teachers, but she did not like sympathy face. She crossed her arms.

Mr. Easton hastily changed the subject. "Actually, I wanted to talk to you about chess club. We're missing you this fall. The other kids, you know, really appreciated that you took the time to work with them on their opening gambits last year, and there's the interscholastic tournament coming up soon so—"

He went on about chess club. Ollie bit her tongue. She wanted to go outside, she wanted to ride her bike, and she didn't want to rejoin chess club.

When Mr. Easton finally came to a stop, she said, not quite meeting his eyes, "I'll send the club some links about opening gambits. Super helpful. They'll work fine. Um, tell everyone I'm sorry."

He sighed. "Well, it's your decision. But if you were to change your mind, we'd love—"

"Yeah," said Ollie. "I'll think about it." Hastily she added, "Gotta run. Have a good day. Bye." She was out the door before Mr. Easton could object, but she could feel him watching her go.

Past the green lockers, thirty-six on each side, down the hall that always smelled like bleach and old sandwiches. Out the double doors and onto the front lawn. All around was bright sun and cool air shaking golden trees: fall in East Evansburg. Ollie took a glad breath. She was going to ride her bike down along the creek as far and as fast as she could go. Maybe she'd jump in the water. The creek wasn't *that* cold. She would go home at dusk—sunset at 5:58. She had lots of time. Her dad would be mad that she got home late, but he was always worrying about something. Ollie could take care of herself.

Her bike was a Schwinn, plum-colored. She had locked it neatly to the space nearest the gate. No one in Evansburg would steal your bike—*probably*—but Ollie loved hers and sometimes people would prank you by stealing your wheels and hiding them.

She had both hands on her bike lock, tongue sticking out as she wrestled with the combination, when a shriek split the air. "It's *mine!*" a voice yelled. "Give it back! No—you can't touch that. NO!"

Ollie turned.

Most of the sixth grade was milling on the front lawn, watching Coco Zintner hop around like a flea—it was she who'd screamed. Coco would not have been out of place in a troop of flower fairies. Her eyes were large, slanting, and ice-blue. Her strawberry-blond hair was so strawberry that in the sunshine it looked pink. You could imagine Coco crawling out of a daffodil each morning and sipping nectar for breakfast. Ollie was a little jealous. She herself had a headful of messy brown curls and no one would ever mistake her for a flower fairy. *But at least,* Ollie reminded herself, *if Phil Greenblatt steals something from me, I'm big enough to sock him.*

Phil Greenblatt had stolen Coco's sparkly notebook. The one Coco had closed when Mr. Easton called on her. Phil was ignoring Coco's attempts to get it back—he was a foot taller than her. Coco was *tiny.* He held the notebook easily over Coco's head, flipped to the page he wanted, and snickered. Coco shrieked with frustration.

"Hey, Brian," called Phil. "Take a look at this."

Coco burst into tears.

Brian Battersby was the star of the middle school

hockey team even though he was only twelve himself. He was way shorter than Phil, but looked like he fit together better, instead of sprouting limbs like a praying mantis. He was lounging against the brick wall of the school building, watching Phil and Coco with interest.

Ollie started to get mad. No one *liked* Coco much—she had just moved from the city and her squeaky enthusiasm annoyed everyone. But really, make her cry in school?

Brian looked at the notebook Phil held out to him. He shrugged. Ollie thought he looked more embarrassed than anything.

Coco started crying harder.

Brian definitely looked uncomfortable. "Come on, Phil, it might not be me."

Mike Campbell said, elbowing Brian, "No, it's totally you." He eyed the notebook page again. "I guess it could be a dog that looks like you."

"Give it *back!*" yelled Coco through her tears. She snatched again. Phil was waving the notebook right over her head, laughing. The sixth grade was laughing too, and now Ollie could see what they were all looking at. It was a picture—a good picture, Coco could really draw—of Brian and Coco's faces nestled together with a heart around them.

Phil sat behind Coco in math class; he must have seen her drawing. Poor dumb Coco—why would you do that if you were sitting in front of nosy Philip Greenblatt?

"Come on, Brian," Mike was saying. "Don't you want to go out with Hot Cocoa here?"

Coco looked like she wanted to run away except that she really wanted her notebook back and Ollie had pretty much had enough of the whole situation, and so she bent down, got a moderate-sized rock, and let it fly.

Numbers and throwing things, those were the two talents of Olivia Adler. She'd quit the softball team last year too, but her aim was still on.

Her rock caught Brian squarely in the back of the head, dropped him *thump* onto the grass, and turned everyone's attention from Coco Zintner to her.

Ideally, Ollie would have hit Phil, but Phil was facing her and Ollie didn't want to put out an eye. Besides, she didn't have a lot of sympathy for Brian. He knew perfectly well that he was the best at hockey, and half the girls giggled about him, and he wasn't coming to Coco's rescue even though he'd more or less gotten her into this with his dumb friends and his dumb charming smile.

Ollie crossed her arms, thought in her mom's voice, *Well, in for a penny . . .*, hefted another rock, and said, "Oops. My hand slipped." The entire sixth grade was staring. The kids in front started backing away. A lot of them thought she had cracked since last year. "Um, seriously, guys," she said. "Doesn't *anyone* have anything better to do?"

Coco Zintner took advantage of Phil's distraction to

snatch her notebook back. She gave Ollie a long look, and darted away.

Ollie thought, *I'm going to have detention for a year,* and then Brian got up, spitting out dirt, and said, "That was a pretty good throw."

The noise began. Ms. Mouton, that day's lawn monitor, finally noticed the commotion. "Now," she said, hurrying over. "Now, now." Ms. Mouton was the librarian and she was not the best lawn monitor.

Ollie decided that she wasn't going to say sorry or anything. Let them call her dad, let them shake their heads, let them give her detention tomorrow. At least tomorrow the weather would change and she would not be stuck in school on a nice day, answering questions.

Ollie jumped onto her bike and raced out of the school yard, wheels spitting gravel, before anyone could tell her to stop.

STAY TUNED
FOR THIS TRIO'S NEXT ADVENTURE,

Dark Waters,

Summer 2021.

Acknowledgments

WRITING A BOOK is not the work of one person. Not really. Only one person types the words, true. But what you don't see when you read a book are the many other people advising, supporting, believing, critiquing. I'd like to thank some of them now.

First and foremost, my editor, Stacey Barney, and her assistant, Caitlin Tutterow, for their incredible patience through the many different iterations of this book. Also to the publicity team for these books, Kathleen Carter, Elyse Marshall, and Jennifer Dee, for the work they put in getting this book out into the world.

To Matt Saunders, most talented of artists, for the splendid cover art, and to Eileen Savage for the design work on this book.

To my agent, Paul Lucas, who got these books out into the world in the first place. And to Eloy Bleifuss and everyone at Janklow and Nesbit, who have done so much for both this series and my career as a whole.

To Vladimir with Mitopeja and Jelena with Dibidus Comics and Books, thank you for being so kind and encouraging about this horror project, and ready to bring the books to audiences in translation.

To the state of Vermont for letting me borrow the winter vibes, and to the staff at the Middlebury College Snow Bowl, likewise. To John, Danya, and everyone at Stone Leaf Teahouse, thanks for letting me put many hours of work in at your tables.

To all the friends who put up with me while I struggled through *Dead Voices*: Garrett for the jokes, RJ for the constant inspiration (whether you knew it or not), and Pollaidh for the jokes about the constant inspiration from RJ. I love you guys.

Thanks to Peter V. Brett and Cassandra Brett for being awesome friends, for reading this series, and for passing copies along. I am so grateful.

To my parents and to my brother, Sterling, thanks so much, guys. You put up with a lot.

And finally, and most importantly, thanks, Evan. You put up with more than anyone when I'm in the middle of writing stuff, and you do it with such grace. I love you.

Born in Austin, Texas, KATHERINE ARDEN spent a year of high school in Rennes, France. Following her acceptance to Middlebury College in Vermont, she deferred enrollment for a year in order to live and study in Moscow. At Middlebury, she specialized in French and Russian literature. After receiving her BA, she moved to Maui, Hawaii, working every kind of odd job imaginable, from grant writing and making crêpes to guiding horse trips. Currently she lives in Vermont, but really, you never know.

You can visit Katherine Arden at katherinearden.com